Baby Father 3:
Does my batty look BIG in this?

Patrick AUGUSTUS

The
X
Press

Published by The X Press
6 Hoxton Square, London N1 6NU
Tel: 0171 729 1199
Fax: 0171 729 1771

Printed by Caledonian International Book Manufacturing Ltd, Glasgow, UK.

Distributed in US by INBOOK, 1436 West Randolph Street, Chicago, Illinois
60607, USA Orders 1-800 626 4330 Fax orders 1-800 334 3892

Distributed in UK by Turnaround Distribution, Unit 3, Olympia Trading Estate,
Coburg Road, London N22 6TZ
Tel: 0181 829 3000
Fax: 0181 881 5088

ISBN 1-874509-57-3

ABOUT THE AUTHOR

Born in south London of Jamaican parents, Patrick Augustus
has worked for many years as a musician and record
producer. As well as being the author of four novels, he has
written and directed several plays, is a regular newspaper,
radio and TV contributor, and a founder member of *The
Baby Fathers Alliance*, a pressure group for separated fathers.
Aged 33, Augustus is currently living in the Canary Islands
where he is writing his next novel.

OTHER BOOKS BY THE AUTHOR

Baby Father
Baby Father 2
When a Man Loves a Woman

This story is about real life and real people. The names, places and
other details have been changed to protect
the innocent, the guilty, and the rest of us.
Patrick Augustus, Ten-a-grief, July 1998

NUFF RESPECT:
Carl Palmer (Jet Star)
who has always been like a father to me. Nuff respect.
Hugh King, my theatre director for all his good advice.
Gammo Speng/Choice FM (London)
Christ Nat, Chris Gray

My promoters:
Lennox Lewis, Ian Wright
Neil Kenlock/Patrick Berry (Choice FM)
Gordon & Keene estate agents (Acre Lane, Brixton) Thompsons
Bakeries, Peppers & Spice, Back To Eden
Mrs Mopp cleaners (0171 737 5855),

The excellent cast of my play 'Baby Father':
Faith, Michael Trojan, Bernadette, Kathy, Carol, Nadine.

Mikey Massive, Pat Griffiths, Sam-I, Junior (Renk Records) Des'ree,
CeCe from Taurus Sound, Cush and Abyssinia.

To all my families and positive ancestors.
ONE LOVE

THE MEN

Gussie Pottinger

Beres Dunkley

Johnny 'Dollar' Lindo

Linvall Henry

ZIM-ZIMMA, WHO GOT THE KEYS TO MY BIMMA?

Those whom the gods wish to destroy, they first make mad amongst themselves...

"But wait, you nuh see how Jah powerful an' great?" Johnny began, scratching his natty dreadlocks. "Look how Him get iron bird inna the sky. Y'know, Him could jus' lick dis yah plane down same way."

Gussie let out a loud groan. The last thing he wanted to hear as the Airbus climbed to 30,000 feet, was that the Creator might, on a whim, cause the plane to crash. He hated flying at the best of times, but he was too embarrassed to admit as much to any of his friends. For one thing, they would probably split their sides laughing. After all, it was an irrational fear, not one that was usually associated with a strong black man — and a Jamaican at that. He had read all the statistics and knew that he was more likely to die in a car crash/of a heart attack/by a crime of passion yet, somehow, he was sure that the odds were against him on this flight. Nothing could convince him otherwise. He knew for a fact that these were his last minutes alive, and that any minute now...

Patrick Augustus

As far as Gussie could see, he was the only one on the plane who was aware of the impending doom. Everybody else seemed to be enjoying the flight. One or two passengers were already asleep, some were reading, others chatted away casually. How could they not sense that the plane was most definitely heading for disaster, Gussie wondered, taking another swig from his hip flask and soaking his fears in more rum.

When his bonafide spars, Johnny, Linvall and Beres, suggested that they all take a holiday together, Gussie was in immediate agreement. A holiday was just what they needed after their women had stitched them up live and direct on the nationally syndicated *Janet Sinclair Show*. Gussie's idea of a holiday, though, was a week up in the Lake District, or walking in the Scottish Highlands. He wouldn't even have minded taking the Euro Star to Paris, or all the way to the French Alps for a skiing holiday. Most definitely.

Seven days and nights of cold weather was, however, definitely not Johnny Dollar's idea of a holiday. Linvall agreed. It wasn't a holiday unless the climate was sultry and there was the possibility of a little adultery. Beres, the uptight buppie, didn't mind where they went as long as he could get the hell out of London for a while. He was still reeling from the indignity of his private life being exposed on TV, his dirty laundry hung out for the whole country to see.

Any discussion of their holiday destination was, in any case, all academic now. Johnny had been unable to resist snapping up the cheapo-cheapo holiday he had seen advertised, and had paid for himself and his

2

friends with his credit card and had billed them subsequently. Seven nights in a self-catering chalet close to the beach. With the strong pound and the low holiday price, they were actually going to be making a profit by spending a week in Tenerife, Johnny reasoned.

Gussie gulped down another shot of rum. St Vincent rum, the strongest in the Caribbean. That was exactly what he needed. The only way he was going to be able to deal with the impending crash was to get smashed out of his head. Most definitely.

Death wouldn't have seemed so inevitable to Gussie if his rastafarian companion wasn't in such philosophical mood. And when it came to rasta philosophy, there was no better master than Johnny Dollar at flexing in and out of rasta doctrine with a potpourri of choice Old Testament 'sound bites' and Jamaican patois.

"Yes, Jah is truly the Almighty," Johnny Dollar continued, taking a bite out of the bun and cheese he had packed for the flight with the certain knowledge that the airline wouldn't be serving up an ital meal. "Bow your heads an' pray. 'Cause if Him want, Jah could just fling two lightning flash an' one massive thunder clap, an' this plane would just drop outta the sky an' crash..."

Even as Johnny spoke, the plane hit severe turbulence and started to shudder. Sweating profusely, Gussie groaned even more loudly and reached for his hip flask yet again. He looked out of the window. On the horizon, a flash of lightning lit up the evening sky. This is it, Gussie was thinking. THIS IS MOST

DEFINITELY IT. The plane's going to crash. Dear Lord, forgive me my sins... Please God, let me live just a little longer... If I had just a bit more time, I would live good. Most definitely. I would live righteous. Just let me live a few more years, Lord. Or even a month more... A week... Another day... Lord, just a few more hours. I'M NOT READY TO DIE!

"See't deh," Johnny pointed to the storm on the horizon. "Out of the hills of Zion comes Jah lightning an' thunder. Jah vengeance surely will come down on anybody, who still insist to stay in wicked babylon. Yes, man, Jah could just blow up this raas plane. Any time."

Cold sweat trickled down from Gussie's newly-shaven bald pate. He tugged at his goatee and groaned again. If only Johnny would refrain from all the negative interaction. But how could he tell him to ease off without exposing his terror of flying? He had no choice but to put on a brave face, and a smile with it. That St. Vincent firewater seemed to be doing the trick, as the slightly moronic grin on his face testified. He drank another mouthful. He was almost inebriated now. Another gulp and he wouldn't feel a thing when the plane came crashing down...

Until the plane departed from Gatwick Airport, the four friends had been happily swapping stories from *A-Z News*, Jamaica's most outrageous newspaper, several copies of which had been sent to Johnny from a relative in Kingston. The stories were hilarious:

JEALOUS DOG BITES MAN'S PENIS
A young man who goes by the name 'Shara' got more than he

bargained for when he paid a recent visit to the house of a lady friend. He was attacked, not by a jealous lover but by a jealous dog, after which 'Shara' needed eighteen stitches to save his severed penis.

According to sources close to the incident, 'Shara' had gone to visit a young married woman on Barnes Road in Montego Bay while her husband was out. Little did 'Shara' know that the maaga dog had been taught by his master to seek and destroy any man who might come to the gate to check his wife whilst he was out. It is understood that the man made the mistake of leaning against the fence when the vicious dog pounced on his private parts.

"The man haffe hol' on 'pon him c**k an' run with him shirt-back full ah wind," said a female neighbour. "From me ah grow up me hear seh a dog is supposed to be a man's best friend... But inna dis yah case, a 'jealous dog' is a angry dog."

Speculation is growing among the local residents that the man's injury might lead to him becoming impotent.

A-Z NEWS, JUNE 23.

Though the others had a good chuckle at it, one story that Johnny was not amused by, concerned a rastaman:

In Jamaica, rastafarians emphasise their discipline to Jah Jah teachings by maintaining a strict diet and often condemning 'baldheads' for eating pig-meat. However, Ras Winston Fearon, 36, told the Portland Court House, where he is on trial on charges of unlawful possession of a female pig, that there is nothing in the scriptures which stated that one can't "teef a pig and make a earning from its sales."

The Dread's comments brought uncontrollable laughter from the packed courtroom.

Also charged with Fearon is Judah Ashman, 39, of 25 Ballas Road, Portland.

The arresting officer, Detective Sergeant 'Round Head' Grant said, on patrolling the Goat Street area, he stopped the two accused as they pushed a handcart. On searching the cart, he discovered a female pig (valued at $3,000), its mouth tightly bound with a bandage. When he challenged the accused, Judah said nothing. Winston 'the natty dread' turned to Judah and said, "Tell the policeman seh ah you teef the pig. I man no deal inna pig. I a 'rasta'."

A-Z NEWS, JUNE 24

Johnny told his friends in no uncertain terms that his faith was something he didn't take for a joke business. "My dreadlocks aren't just a fashion statement, you know. And anyway, not every 'ras' is a rasta. In Jamaica, you have rasta, ras-*cal* and raas-*claat*. Skeen?"

The humorous pages of *A-Z News* kept the four amused as they sat in the departure lounge of the airport waiting to board their flight. By the time the Airbus was taxiing down the runway, Johnny had begun to get deep and spiritual.

Johnny Dollar hadn't been the same since the *Janet Sinclair Show*. None of them had. After the humiliation they had suffered at the hands of Janet Sinclair, no black man could have been expected to be the same person afterwards as he was prior to it. The others assumed that the pressure must have really got to Johnny when he had insisted on carrying his entire collection of miniature Gideon Bibles on the plane as hand luggage. Some people collect records, others collect expired car tax discs. Johnny had collected Bibles ever since his nyabinghi days, and whenever someone he knew was going to hospital or staying in a hotel, he always put in a request for the free Bible on the bedside table.

Johnny Dollar, the 'original baby father', had featured in many embarrassing situations over the years, such was the precarious life of a man who had to juggle between different baby mothers, just to make sure that his pickney were well taken care of. But nothing in his wayward life had prepared him for what was to happen on the *Janet Sinclair Show*. That he and his three spars had been well and truly shafted by a feminist mafia consisting of Janet Sinclair herself and her guests — their own partners — was transparent.

For one thing, he had been invited on the popular talk show to discuss 'male bonding', yet they hardly touched on the subject. Instead, Janet Sinclair introduced the live studio audience to Sharon, who revealed that she was about to become Johnny's baby mother number three. Live on national television! Johnny almost collapsed. He couldn't believe it. This renk gal, who he had obliged with a little slap and tickle/bump and grind in the back room of The Book Shack, the Peckham bookstore that he ran, decided to tell him that she was pregnant on Brixton's favourite terrestrial television show. The question was whether he would ever be able to show his face on the streets of south London again.

It was just a one night stand. As far as Johnny was

concerned, he was doing her a favour. That's the kind of sensitive black man that he was. He just couldn't bear to know that a single sista had been living alone for years without any real sex to write home about. With the world-renowned shortage of black men, he felt it only right to share himself amongst all those thousands of lonely sistas. Sharon should have been grateful, instead she repaid his generosity by revealing to all and sundry that Johnny Dollar was about to become a statistic once more, and that she was yet another reason for the Child Support Agency to distress him.

After the show, Johnny had to keep a distinctively low profile. Lesley, his number one baby mother, had not seen the show live, but Johnny had quickly got word through the ghetto grapevine that someone had bumped into Lesley and that one word led to another, "*Reh-reh-reh*... I saw Johnny 'pon TV last night an'... *reh-reh-reh*...*"* After the way that he had been trying to get back 'up close and personal' with her of late, the news that yet another woman was about to give birth to a child for which Johnny donated the sperm was not likely to go down too well. So Johnny had done the honourable thing and left a note at home for Lesley saying that he had gone on an important fishing trip for a couple of weeks and that he really loved her, and wasn't it amazing how much idle 'su-su' there was on the streets nowadays with any and everybody chatting everyone else's business and that he, for one, never listened to gossip. Then he went and holed up at Beres' house for the next seven days.

A new baby, by yet another woman... Johnny had to

think carefully about how he was going to play this one. He had no choice but to get outta town for a while, because if Lesley already knew about it, it was only a matter of time before Lesley's mother would hear about it and, after the last time, she had warned him about what she would do to him with a meat cleaver the next time he fathered a child by a woman other than her daughter. Yes, he definitely had to get outta town. Lesley's entire family were probably seething at home right now, watching his TV debut over a plate of rice and peas.

Johnny sighed. He desperately needed to clear his head of all the madness of his domestic life — something he should have done a long time ago. What better way to sort out your life than by lying on a sunny beach surrounded by a trailerload of topless beauties? Desperate problems required desperate solutions and, this time, Johnny needed to come up with his best excuse EVER. Even that might not save his relationship with Lesley. When an excuse had to be that good, it was best to fly out to somewhere like Tenerife, where you could kick back and relax with your bonafide bredrin and the aforementioned world-a-girls, just to be able to compose the right words.

Now, when Johnny looked out of the window of the Airbus into the darkening sky, he felt a natural mystic in the air. Not since he had last been to a nyabinghi gathering had he felt such a spiritual power. It was as if he was truly seeing the beauty of God's creation for the first time, and in that beauty there was a truth, and that truth was the answer to the fundamental questions of life: Who are we? What are we? Should man live by one woman alone?

Johnny turned to his Bible, looking for guidance and assurance. As if by divine intervention, the pages opened at Deutronomy 5, The Ten Commandments:

Do not commit adultery.

The words seemed to jump out of the page and slap him hard across the face.

Do not commit adultery.

Still reeling from the slap, Johnny closed his eyes and opened them again.

Do not commit adultery.

He looked out of the window and turned back to the Bible.

Do not commit adultery.

He closed the Bible and opened it again arbitrarily. The page fell on Deutronomy 5 again.

Do not commit adultery.

Johnny began to sweat. Even with his eyes closed and the book shut, the words were still ringing in his ears.

Baby Father 3: *Does my batty look big in this?*

Do not commit adultery!

Do not commit adultery!

Do not commit adultery!

Do not commit adultery!

He tried to run away from the words.

Do not commit adultery!

Do not commit adultery!

Do not commit adultery!

Do not commit adultery!

In his mind he ran as fast as he could and just kept running, back to his childhood memories:

As far back as he could remember, Johnny had always known that there was something different about him. Even when he was at school, he realized that he was not the same as other boys. The teachers often came up to him in the changing rooms after the P.E. class and, looking him up and down as he showered, would ask whether he was really only twelve years old. Even though Raymond Banton and the other kids would laugh, Johnny really didn't understand what the big deal was. In fact, he became embarrassed about how well endowed he was, too embarrassed to check girls when all his mates were getting their first taste of female flesh.

Instead of spending his time learning the fine and very delicate art of 'chirpsing gal', Johnny became a voracious consumer of academic books. He was a brilliant student. First Class in mathematics and the sciences, and the teachers always hoped that he would go on to university a year early. There was even talk of him taking the Oxbridge exams and going on to great things. He thought back and remembered how confident he was in those days. Indeed, he was so full of himself that he even believed he was going to rule the world one day.

Those were the good old days, the innocent days, when he had a bright future ahead of him. Before he got introduced to a world-a-girls.

Do not commit adultery!

He didn't remember much about that summer. By the second day of the summer holidays, school was usually well and truly banished from teenage minds. Johnny was the only sixteen year old who looked forward to spending the six weeks solving mathematical problems. But this was also the summer he discovered raving. He even developed a little bounce in his step when he walked with a white towel hanging out of his back pocket and an afro comb sticking out of the back of his thick, bushy, Jackson 5-size afro. Those were the good old days, the innocent days, just before he relinquished his bright future.

Baby Father 3: *Does my batty look big in this?*

Once he lost his virginity, there was no stopping him. He couldn't get enough. Word quickly got around to the local female population that here was a brotha hung like he was from another planet. After that, it was like every gal in south London was mad over him. One or two big old women, too.

He didn't stop to think of whether it was the sex that he couldn't resist, or just the idea of conquest. Even when the gals drained him dry, he was having too good a time to stop and think about anything.

By the end of the next school term, Johnny discovered that you can't spend your time chirpsing women and still hope to end up at Oxford or Cambridge University. His grades started falling, and it was with great difficulty that he scraped through his A-Levels at all. From then on, he became just another 'could have been great' black man who never realized his potential.

Now, twenty years later, on his way to a week of fun and frolics in the sun, Johnny wished those days of potential were back again. He scratched his natty dreadlocks as he thought back to those good old days of Mackeson stout and Ford Capris, and wished he had never discovered women at all. If he had kept his mind on his studies, no woman would have been able to go chatting his business on national television. Sistas nowadays were well out of order. He admired all those men who were determined to stay in their relationships until 'death do us part'. He didn't know how they did it, but he saluted their ability to stay in a relationship for so long without anybody getting killed.

"Excuse me, sir…"

Johnny looked up to see a beautiful ebony-coloured princess smiling down at him. He responded with his most charming 'undercover lover' smile.

Do not commit adultery!

"...Sir, would you fasten your safety belt," the stewardess said. "The Captain has still not switched off the 'fasten seatbelt' sign, due to all this turbulence."

Johnny complied immediately. As the stewardess continued her journey down the narrow aisle unsteadily, he called her back.

"By the way," he said casually, extending his hand, "my name is Johnny Dollar. Back in Brixton they call me 'Mr. Loverman'."

The stewardess continued smiling her corporate 'customer is always right' smile. As the only black stewardesses on the airline, she was used to the occasional male passenger chatting her up. Suddenly, a look of recognition darkened her face.

"Wait a minute, weren't you on the *Janet Sinclair Show* last week? Yes, it's you, isn't it? You're that Johnny Dollar."

"The one and the same," Johnny said, bigging up his chest proudly.

"If you take my advice, sir, you're too girlie-girlie. You must learn to fasten your safety belt and keep your chastity belt locked."

With that she sashayed down the aisle unsteadily, her corporate smile still in place.

"That will teach you, Johnny," Linvall laughed from

across the aisle. "You're too fast, guy."

Do not commit adultery!

Johnny grinned uncomfortably. Sex was his one temptation. Could he really not keep his mind off it for more than ten seconds…? Ten, nine, eight, seven, sex, five, four, three…

Do not commit adultery!

That's how it had been ever since that summer of his sixteenth birthday. He remembered that he had a permanent stiffie almost the entire summer. Sometimes it would rise up before him and wake him from his slumber with a tug and a, "Good morning, Johnny, I'm going out to play today, fancy coming with me?" As if he had a choice.

Since that summer, Johnny and his penis had had a really intimate relationship. They often discussed Marx and nuclear fission with one another and supported each other as best they could. In fact, so attached were this man and his manhood that Johnny had followed willy-nilly to his doom on more than one occasion, yet somehow survived. It was a case of the dog leading its owner by the leash.

Do not commit adultery!

Johnny stared at the dark sky outside, wondering why he had got himself into this mess in the first place. Being

15

a baby father wasn't as blissful as it was cracked up to be. A quick inventory of his life as a 'pappa', revealed a catalogue of deviousness and deceit between himself and any number of women. The amount of time he had wasted juggling between one and the other... He could have been spending that time on something more productive, like the hot pursuit of cash money. Weren't people always reminding him about how much talent he had? Yet, while he spent his time encouraging youngsters to make the most of the opportunities that came their way he had, regretfully, not applied the philosophy to his own life. What had he done with the gift that the man upstairs had given him? What did he have to show for it? Nothing. Nothing, but 'x' amount of kids by 'x' amount of different women. When he looked back on his life, the one talent he seemed to have made the most of was the ability to breed. That hardly distinguished him from 'x' amount of men out there.

What had become of all his dreams, hopes and ambitions? Could he still rule the world, he wondered. Maybe. Anything was possible if he didn't have baby father commitments. Wherever he turned, he had baby mothers baying for his blood, not to talk of children to clothe and feed. As his thoughts roamed, Johnny couldn't help wondering what it would be like to be free and single again.

"Blouse an' skirt!" he exclaimed suddenly, like Archimides in the bathtub. The plane was literally being tossed from side to side by the turbulence. "Me nuh tell you seh Jah great? You must nevah tek Jah business fe a joke business, y'know. Every baldhead should respect the rastaman. Because Jah seh no bird can fly without flapping its wings, an' me nevah yet see dis yah iron bird even move its wings," he told his companions and anyone else who cared to listen. "All ah unuh with your calculators, calculate your judgement. Jah seh the thunder is going to be seven times heavier than the last time. Dat mean to say, him could fling dis yah plane down — any time! Skeen?"

Gussie groaned like a condemned man.

To Johnny, it was clear, if his penis had not been divorced from his morals at such an early age he might have made something of his life. Instead, he didn't even own a home to show for his efforts. Everybody knew that a man without a home was like a dog without a bone.

Beres was also in deep contemplation. He fingered his pinstripe moustache and readjusted his gold-rimmed spectacles instinctively. Why had he allowed himself to be set up as he had been on the *Janet Sinclair Show?* How could his wife, Caroline, embarrass him on coast to coast television by announcing that she was to become his ex-wife and then parade her new boyfriend in front of the cameras to add insult to injury? It had all come as one big surprise to him.

How could a woman be that devious?. How could Caroline totally demolish his image as the renaissance black man who knew how to treat his partner right, and who (almost) always did the right thing? Devious was the right word for it. If she hadn't been so devious, she wouldn't have noticed that his underpants were back to front when he returned from his illicit liaison.

It was the first time he had ever been unfaithful to a woman. At least Caroline could have taken that into consideration. Okay, he was still wrong to have done it, but there were mitigating circumstances which, to a lawyer like Caroline, should have been sufficient grounds for clemency. For one thing, she was spending so much time working in Brussels that he could hardly have been blamed for straying this one time. Besides, the woman he got off with was his first wife, Sonia, and Sonia was practically gay anyway. So it didn't count — so to speak.

Unlike his friends, Beres wasn't going to Tenerife for the opportunity of bedding lots of women. Just one would do. If he could find the right woman, who knows, he might forget that Caroline ever existed. Besides, this break was long overdue. He rarely found time in his hectic buppie life to take a proper holiday. If he had taken a holiday when he was feeling frustrated about Caroline's long distance commuting to the European Courts of Justice in Belgium, maybe he would still be regarded as the ultimate renaissance black man, instead of being categorized, on the *Janet Sinclair Show,* alongside the likes of Johnny Dollar who, after all, was a serial baby father.

Beres had fond memories of Tenerife. That was where he had met Sonia eight years ago. This return trip, would be an opportunity to come to terms with the prospect of his life being shattered by a second divorce. The only way he could deal with the pain of having lost a fundamental part of himself — his woman — was to get his groove back.

If you're not weeping and wailing people think you're doing all right. His friends thought that Beres was ever as solid as a rock, despite his wrecked marriage, and he had no intention of informing them otherwise — that he was devastated inside. Men just didn't allow other men to get that close to their emotions. Moreover, they would probably laugh at the fact that he was grieving so heavily over the loss of his woman. When he looked across at each of his three travelling companions, he couldn't see any of them being able to understand how much it meant to him to save his marriage. When he thought about it now, that's exactly what he wanted to do. In point of fact, he would even abstain from bedding any women on this trip if he knew for sure that Caroline would come back to him.

Unlike Johnny, Linvall and Gussie, Beres had always tried his best to do the right thing. There were so very few successful buppie marriages that he felt as if the whole of the black community was watching his marriage and he didn't want to let them down. He wanted to be proof that successful upwardly mobile black couples did exist and that their marriages did work out, albeit with great difficulty and personal sacrifice. But it wasn't just that, he didn't want to separate from Caroline because he was really in love with her. Just as he had been with Sonia.

He had always been a one woman man, and if it was up to him he and Sonia would never have split up in the first place. He still felt guilty about the breakdown of his first marriage, even though the most militant fundamentalist feminist would agree that he had made a good effort. He provided Sonia with everything a wife could ask for: a loving husband and father who worked hard to provide his wife and daughter with all the little luxuries of life — a house of substantial proportions in one of the most desirable streets in south London, a brand new Mercedes in the driveway and a string of gold and platinum credit cards. Okay, so he worked all the hours God sent to maintain the buppie lifestyle, but it wasn't his fault that Sonia had decided that she preferred women to men. She said she needed to discover "The real me", and that she needed to "find" herself again.

After seven years of marriage he thought he was doing all right. He still put every effort into making their nights together seem like that very first night in Tenerife. How was he to know that love had long been well and truly buried? In court, during the custody battle, Sonia had been brilliant at reeling off his 894 failings, but it was the first he had heard of it. Was she really talking about the same marriage he had spent the last seven years in?

If it was up to Beres, he and Caroline would not be getting divorced either. Like most buppies, he held a traditional view of marriage and the family. As far as he was concerned, you made your commitments for life and then stuck by them — for richer or poorer. Okay, he had made a mistake the first time, and maybe both marriages were a mistake, he couldn't be sure (it was a lot easier to see what had gone wrong with his car showroom business than his marriage), but he was damned if he was going to simply stand by and become just another 'married and divorced twice' statistic. No way. As he sat through the turbulence, Beres determined not to give up his marriage without a fight.

Compared to the others, the *Janet Sinclair Show* handled Linvall lightly. Unlike them, he wasn't exposed to the world as a cheat. Considering his past, that was a result. The price you paid, as a fashion photographer, for jetsetting around taking pictures of the world's most beautiful women, was to be led blindly to temptation (it was a high price to pay but, Linvall accepted, a worthwhile price considering the brilliant photographs he got as a result). He was a trendy 'cool Britannia' photographer sporting funki dreds and dressed from head to toe in Moschino, with charm and an inviting smile above his perfect goatee. It wasn't his fault that those were, coincidentally, the essential ingredients for sex around the clock. He couldn't help it, that was the way it was. Why, he had even been voted one of the ten best dressed man in London by one of the upmarket women's fashion magazines.

While not suffering the same indignity as his friends, Linvall was nevertheless incensed that his wife Marcia had not desisted from maligning his image as one of the most happening photographers in London (as voted by one of the upmarket style magazines last year). He couldn't afford to be made to look like a pussywhipped 'maama man' in front of millions of TV viewers. Talk about character assassination, Janet Sinclair and his wife were taking the frigging liberties! Why didn't they just shoot him up with lead right there and then? If there was one thing he wasn't, it was pussywhipped. He was a strong, hard-as-nails brotha, how could he be pussywhipped? It was only because of their son that he had ever agreed to get back with Marcia. It didn't have anything to do with whip appeal.

Linvall just couldn't understand how Marcia could go on national television and tell the world that living with him had taught her that all men were dogs and, therefore, must be kept on a short leash. Yeah, *right*. Like she could restrain him with a leash. How could she have talked about their relationship like that? He couldn't even get a word in edgeways in his own defence, it was like Janet Sinclair was controlling the microphone and making sure it never reached over to the men's side. Anyway, he reasoned, it would have been difficult to defend himself with the largely female audience hissing at him throughout.

Now he was a laughing stock. He couldn't even go into the public lavatories at the airport without someone looking up from the pissoire and recognizing him immediately: " 'Ere, you're that pussywhipped geezer, ain'tcha?"

Everywhere he went women made whip-cracking noises and the fellas 'miaowed' loudly. He even had one youth stop him at the traffic lights and say, "Bwoy, me nuh really like to see a black man look like dat 'pon TV, yuh know. Me nearly fling a bottle through my television set... To see a pussywhipped black man stand up 'pon TV an' nuh do not'n fe defend himself. Black men like you give the rest of us a bad name."

Linvall seethed with anger when he thought that Marcia had only given him permission to go on this trip with the strict understanding that he was to take snapshots, so that she could see that he hadn't spent the holiday chirpsing girls, but had gone sightseeing instead. That was the last thing he intended to do. This holiday was going to be seven sultry nights in the sun. He hadn't even got there yet and already he had a hard-on.

Family life had become like a ball made of heavy duty lead chained to his testicles, it was painful and filled with distress — hardly an atmosphere conducive to enhancing a man's virility. As a quiet and sedate family man, every day was the same as the day before, and bedtime came at eleven-thirty every night.

Meditating on the subject of family life, Linvall came to the conclusion that women get the best deal out of relationships. As long as a man remains a bachelor, the balance of power remains with him. The woman will do anything just to maintain the possibility of being able to tie him down some time in the distant future. But from the moment a man says 'I do', it's all over, the goal posts have shifted, the relationship needs redefining and, guess who's cracking the whip now? Yep, Linvall concluded, every family man needs a regular week's holiday on the razzle with the lads, just to stay sane. He was going to enjoy playing away from home. He was going to make the most of it. He had every intention of checking the most amount of women, because he couldn't be sure of when the opportunity would come again.

They had now been in turbulence for two hours. Gussie was feeling desperate. Most definitely. The plane was being tossed about like it was a dinghy on a stormy sea with gale force winds. Gussie actually started feeling seasick. "Just don't throw up," he kept telling himself. "Just don't throw up." He hadn't felt this sick since the *Janet Sinclair Show*. And since the show he had been sick many times, because it had shattered his nerves so much that all he had been able to do since then was eat chocolates (boxes and boxes of the stuff) and drink (gallons and gallons of different brews). He had put on so much weight in the week since the show that his clothes didn't fit him any more and he had been forced to make a hurried trip to GAP to purchase a set of khakis and a light summer suit — the baggier the better.

He wouldn't have been on the show at all if he hadn't agreed to become a surrogate father because of a shortage of cash. But he had needed to save his jewellery shop. He couldn't let everybody see him go bankrupt because of what he owed the tax man. The banks were refusing to lend him any money. In fact his bank manager actually laughed in his face when he came in and asked to borrow 'x' amount of grands. That was the biggest humiliation. Gussie hadn't even realised that it was April 1st, but Mr O'Flaherty, the bank manager, naturally assumed that he was having a laugh. "You can't make a monkey out of me," O'Flaherty said with a wink of his eye.

Gussie had no choice but to donate his sperm for cash. Plus he got to sleep with a TV personality who he had wanted to check for a long time. That was the icing on the cake. It was like a double whammy: a celebrity lay, and the cash came in handy, too.

Gussie was confident that he would never have any emotional attachment with the issue of his contractual liaison with Angela Braithwaite, but when she was introduced on the *Janet Sinclair Show* and told everybody that she was expecting his twins, that nearly killed him. It wrecked his imminent marriage to weather girl Winsome Scott, and he was made to look like any old wotless and irresponsible black man with women all over the place.

Gussie just couldn't figure out why it was, that the harder he tried to get married the more unsuccessful he became. Okay, he had previously judged a woman by looking at her beautiful body, but in the past year he had made every effort to take their charm, personality and intellect into consideration, yet he had still come a cropper. Women were always talking about the world-renowned shortage of black men. Well, here he was, one of the most eligible black men in London. He was handsome, trim, intelligent, and he ran a jewellery shop in Hatton Garden. You couldn't get much more eligible than that. He should have been the envy of all his friends and the dream of women everywhere but, instead, Janet Sinclair had made him look like he was prepared to hire his dick out to the highest bidder.

Why were all the good girls already taken? Why did he keep falling for hard headed women? He couldn't think straight. When you're as drunk as he was by now, you don't make sense to yourself. He was so drunk, there was nothing else to do but cry as he thought about the sorry state he was in. Tears streamed down his cheeks as he recalled the many times women had used and abused him, though in the case of his ex-wife the woman was a man. Gussie could think of no worse nightmare than to end up marrying a woman who used to be a man. But that's exactly what happened to him. Now he had sold his twins for thirty pieces of silver... Could life get any worse? He sobbed like a baby.

Maybe his problem was that he kept falling in love too easily, he considered. Yes, maybe that was it. He had to stop falling in love at first sight. From now on things would be different. He wasn't going to get caught out again. As far as he was concerned, love didn't live here any more. Most definitely not.

He sobbed some more.

From where he sat across the aisle, Johnny thought that Gussie was laughing.

"Blouse an' skirt!" he exclaimed. "You dread, yah know Gussie. Jah ah fling aeroplane about inna the sky an' you ah siddung an' a laugh. You mussi drunk, star."

Piss off, Johnny, Gussie was thinking. Don't distress me when I'm trying to stop from puking.

"Eh Gussie, you better not drink any more of that rum, y'know," Johnny continued. "Remember that time when you were so drunk — we was all drunk — and you stuck your arm up an elephant's arse in London Zoo? Don't you remember that?"

The Captain's voice came over the speakers:

"We are experiencing some turbulence. Nothing to worry about..."

Despite all the captain's reassuring words, the turbulence didn't subside. Far from it. It seemed to be getting worse. The plane felt like it was passing through a tornado as it was tossed from side to side like a feather in the sky. Gussie was already too sloshed to care, but many of the other passengers were now at their wits end. The plane had experienced turbulence for two and a half hours without respite. Even the bravest of passengers, who had flown hundreds of times, began to wonder if they would ever reach their destination. Nobody had ever experienced a flight as rough as this. The longer the turbulence continued, the louder became their anxious voices, and Johnny Dollar's wonderment at the power of the Almighty.

"Dreadlocks sent down a babylon to warn the nation, tell them 'bout how Jah powerful an' great. Jah so powerful, him could jus' fling dis yah plane down. So if you diss Marcus, you must bite the dust, an' if you diss Selassie I, you shall surely die. It says so right yah so inna de Bible, from Genesis right through to Revelations, skeen?"

Then Johnny started chanting the rasta man chant:

> *Jah got the whole world in his hands*
> *Jah got the whole wide world in his hands*
> *Jah got the whole world in his hands*
> *Jah got the whole world in his hands...*

The elderly white couple in the row in front were now even whiter with fear. It's a fascinating thing that, as certain doom approaches, even those who have only spent the obligatory births, deaths and marriages in church suddenly ask for a Bible, as if in their last few minutes alive they could repent all their sins. The couple turned around to Johnny and asked if they could borrow his Bible, if only briefly.

Johnny didn't seem surprised, but he told them that he needed his Bible himself. However, if they had twenty pounds on them, he could sell them one of the back-up Bibles he had carried on board as hand luggage.

At a time like this, twenty pounds didn't seem at all excessive for the fountain of wisdom. In fact the white couple regarded it as positively a bargain in the circumstances. They eagerly handed Johnny a crisp twenty pound note and, with more than a little urgency, hungrily thumbed the pages of the miniature Gideon Bible he handed them.

Johnny pocketed the cash and loudly continued his philosophising on Jah's power and might.

"If Jah decide to fling one lightning clap an' mek dis plane crash, no covetous or gravilicious weakheart on board will survive. Skeen? Your calculators won't save you. Your birth cerfi-ticket won't save you, neither. 'Cause the hotter the battle, the sweeter Jah victory. It is easier for a camel to pass through a needle's eye than for a rich man to enter into Zion. Remember, Jah promised the earth to the meek. Skeen?"

Now though, Johnny's sermon was not falling on deaf ears. What he was saying seemed to have a lot of truth as the pilot searched in vain for turbulent-free air pockets. Under the circumstances, nearly everybody on board felt compelled to give praises unto Jah and declare that He really was the Almighty and that He had the power to fling down this plane at any minute, though they prayed that he would refrain from exercising his prerogative on this particular flight.

What they all needed at a time like this was a Bible. It didn't take long for word to filter amongst the passengers that Johnny Dollar was the only one on the flight with a seemingly endless supply of Bibles. Within minutes he was selling handfuls of his free Gideon Bibles at twenty pounds a throw. Everybody agreed that it was a bargain, considering. Money was passed back from row to row as Johnny was inundated with orders. "Give unto Caesar what is due unto Caesar," he declared as people dipped into their wallets. From every direction, money was coming towards him.

"Dem ah fly go ah Jupiter an' fly go ah Mars, all dem ah fly an' dem still cyant touch the sky. You nuh see how Jah powerful an' mighty. Him could jus' lick down dis aeroplane, an' everybody on board — the rich an' poor, the good and the bad, the high an' the low is in his hands. Jah got the whole wide world in his hands. Selassie I know dat!"

Beres had never seen anything like it before. As the cabin crew looked on bemused, Johnny led old biddies and young ones alike in a nyabinghi chant praising Jahovia. The chanting had succeeded in distracting the passengers from the turbulence, which was tossing the plane around even more violently now. This impromptu revival meeting was a godsend and, for the moment, the crew had no intention of terminating these upfront rasta man chants:

Keep cool babylon you don't know what you're sayin'
Keep cool babylon you don't know what you're doin'
Keep cool babylon you don't know what you're sayin'
King rasta coming home soon.

If it was a skank, then it was a bloody good one. Johnny had come on board with a hundred Bibles and he had managed to sell them all, making a tidy profit. He insisted to his friends that that was the way Jah Jah planned it. He claimed he had brought the Bibles with him because he didn't want to be without one on this holiday and, just in case the other ninety-nine were mislaid...

Beres still wasn't convinced, but had to accept that Johnny couldn't have predicted the turbulence.

"Still," said Johnny with a gold-capped toothy smile, counting his takings as the plane touched down at Tenerife airport, "I've got the feeling that this is holiday is going to be nice. It only just begin an' me feel irie already, but it nuh finish, it nuh finish, it nuh finish..."

BOO-YAKKA!

If Johnny had known that there wasn't going to be any customs at Tenerife airport, he would have packed some prime sensi in his luggage. He felt like kicking himself when he realized.

Outside, a tropical evening breeze greeted them.

"Tenerife nuh nice like Jamaica nice," Johnny declared, as the four friends piled into a Mercedes-Benz taxi which took them to their destination in the tourist resort of Playa de Las Americas. Johnny had booked a week at the Las Vinas self-catering holiday complex. They were to share a four-bedroom chalet in its exclusive compound. As the taxi sped along the coast road, Gussie, on the back seat fast asleep, snored loudly.

After a fifteen minute drive they arrived at the big hotels of Playa de Las Americas where, it seemed, half of Britain was also in residence sporting various degrees of suntan. Every shade of white skin was represented: brilliant white, off-white, anaemic, lobster-pink, light-tanned, heavy-tanned, chocolate and damn near black.

"An' dem have the dyam nerve fe call WE coloured," Johnny observed with a kiss of his teeth.

Fortunately, Las Vinas wasn't in the heart of Playa de Las Americas. The compound was situated where most tourists would consider 'off the beaten track'. Its grey

Patrick Augustus

walls juxtaposed against the bright green paintwork on the doors, windows, drainpipes, gates and everything else that wasn't concrete. Within the large complex were a mixture of chalets and flats which were rented out to the self-catering holiday maker and tour guides residing permanently on the island.

They had picked up their keys, and were shown to their quarters. Inside number 41 Las Vinas, the four friends inspected the impressive chalet they were to call home for the next seven days and argued over who would have which bedroom. Downstairs, there was a large living room with huge glass doors which opened out onto a little patio facing the communal gardens and swimming pool of the compound. There was also a large kitchen/diner and a shower with toilet. Upstairs, there were four reasonably large bedrooms and another bathroom. There were no carpets on the tiled floors, as was the custom in many sunny climes.

Now they were in Tenerife, there was no time to waste. One by one, they each jumped into the shower then got changed into casuals to go down and explore the town centre. Men always go on about how long women take to get ready, but four guys together on holiday take as much time putting on the finishing touches. Each of them had a toiletries bag as big as an old lady's shopping bag, and spent hours before they felt confident enough to step out into the streets.

"Do you think my batty looks big in this?" Gussie asked Linvall, modelling his new trousers in front of the mirror, just before they departed.

Linvall smirked. "Your batty looks big in anything.

Baby Father 3: *Does my batty look big in this?*

Trust me. The amount of weight that you're putting on, it's not your batty you should be worried about, it's your balls. They must be weighing you down."

Gussie cut Linvall a look that told him that he didn't think that was very funny, and that he would pay Linvall back for that.

Johnny was more concerned in the bald patch at the back of his head which was a sign of the passing of the years. He had spent an hour in front of a mirror in the bathroom trying to cover the patch with a layer of dreadlocks. He prayed that no big wind would come to embarrass him while they were out on the town.

"On the way here in the taxi, me sight two fat dawtas in batty riders," Johnny told his friends. "An' me well waan check them. Skeen? If we hurry we might still be able to catch up with them. When fat gal ah wear batty rider, me haffe inna dat!"

At the first mention of checking gal, Gussie sobered up. As tired as he was, he didn't want to miss out on any action. It was time to get busy.

What Gussie, Johnny, Beres and Linvall considered 'casual' was what most women would call 'dressed to kill'. They strolled down the main boulevard of Playa de Las Americas in light summer suits, a shine on their faces, wearing wraparound shades, looking 'the bizness', ready to shock out and sting. After showering and shaving, they had each splashed on their individual 'lady-killing' colognes on their cheeks, behind their ears and in their crotches (for good luck) and now left a scented trail behind as they walked purposefully amongst the Geordie accents, Scousers, Yorkshiremen

33

and pot-bellied Scotsmen on holiday. The streets were buzzing. The whole place looked and felt like the seafront at Blackpool on a summer's day — bright lights everywhere, and with a pub, restaurant or club on every corner. Most of the holidaymakers couldn't help turning their heads to take a second look at this quartet of black men on the move. The ladies loved what they saw and wished they could dress up their fellas equally elegantly. Linvall, Beres, Johnny and Gussie also loved what they saw from behind their darkers.

"Me coming hot this year, what dem ah go do fe hold me?" Johnny called out loud to anyone who was willing to listen.

"Me coming hotter than hot this year, not even water can cold me."

There were bikini-clad women from all over the world exposing their merchandise for all to see. There were Dutch women, German, Swedish, French and even Russian, and a couple of black mampie queens in batty riders.

"Unuh get me hot, unuh get me wicked," Johnny told the pair of heavyweight sistas, as he stepped in their path, tugging at his crotch. "Naomi Campbell nuh pretty like unuh."

"Piss of!" said one of them in a deep, masculine voice.

"Batty man ah wear batty rider! Ah wha' de bumboclaat ah gwan?" Johnny said, taking of his sunglasses to see if he was imagining things.

Their first watering hole was a pub run by Terry, a white skinhead from Bermondsey in his mid-thirties.

Baby Father 3: *Does my batty look big in this?*

He had insisted on serving the four black friends free beers when he saw them strolling past his establishment. He explained to them that he had been a hardcore reggae fanatic since his youth and, as far as he was concerned we are all 'bredrin'.

"Blimey, when I was fourteen I used to follow Saxon sound system, wiv Papa Levi, Daddy Rusty, Smiley Culture and Tippa Irie," Terry explained, as he plied his new-found friends with another round of drinks. Followed them all over London. It was a right larf. I used to roll a big fat spliff and stand by the speaker all night. I didn't give a toss that I was the only white boy. Remember Papa Levi...? *'Me black me no white, arrive at the dance...' "*

Johnny Dollar couldn't believe that a white guy could chat lyrics so good. In fact, only a handful of deejays could chat the fast style originated by Peter King of the Saxon crew, without pausing for breath. He gave Terry props by saluting him with a touch of his fists.

Johnny had to touch Terry's fist several more times that evening, as it became apparent that Terry KNEW his music. He went behind the bar to pull out a selection of tunes. Johnny was forced to say "Respect in every aspect," as one vintage tune after another floated out through the speakers — vintage Al Green, 'double vintage' Aretha Franklin, Otis Redding, Marvin Gaye and many more stars from yesteryear. Terry even had a few 'specials' which only he possessed.

"Where the raas you get these tunes from?" Johnny asked.

Patrick Augustus

Terry had apparently been a deejay for years. He had even played at several black weddings and was one of the coolest white guys any of them had met.

"The first black wedding I did, they didn't even know I was white, because they had only heard me spinning records on my old pirate radio show, when I used to be known as DJ Black Amabassador. So I turned up there and, blimey, they've got these two geezers, the size of elephants, on the door and they turn round to me and say, 'Not tonight, sunshine.' I suppose the wedding wasn't a caucasian occasion, know what I mean? But when I started dropping tunes, the whole place sparked up. I got another couple of black weddings as a result of that gig and, from there, it just took off. Blimey, at one time it looked like I was playing at every black wedding in south London."

From his musical selection, Johnny could hear just why Terry would have been popular.

"Come on lads, drink up. Have another beer, it's on the house," Terry insisted.

He explained that he was a fifth generation Millwall fan, but was willing to concede that Ian Wright had scored many (in his words) "BOO-YAKKA" goals. He and his wife, Sylvia, had fallen in love with Tenerife after visiting on holiday several years back. They decided almost immediately to stay and work for one of the many English bar owners on the island. What was there to stay in England for but miserable weather and lack of opportunity, Terry reasoned. They didn't even need to learn any Spanish beyond a couple of words like 'pesetas'. "Playa de Las Americas is a far off green field

36

that will forever be England," Terry said proudly pointing to the Union Jack next to the portrait of the queen on the wall of his bar. "English is the national language of this part of Tenerife, whatever the Spaniards might be thinking. Blimey, if you can't speak English over here, you must be a foreigner!" Terry laughed so loudly that he nearly lost his balance.

It did seem true that this part of Tenerife had been co-opted into the British Empire. Most of the holidaymakers on the busy promenade outside seemed to be English. It wasn't until much later that Johnny and his friends would discover that the indigenous population of Canary Islanders weren't too happy about that state of affairs. No sah, not at all.

Terry and Sylvia had now worked their way up to managing the Traveller's Retreat pub and were doing very well, thank you. Terry's one regret was that you didn't see a lot of black faces down in Tenerife.

"I want you guys to treat this pub like a home from home whilst you're here," Terry said passing around another tray of free beers. "Consider yourselves my bonafide bredrin..."

After a few more drinks at the Traveller's Retreat, the four friends decided to go on a pub crawl. They had more than enough of a choice. Playa de Las Americas offered every kind of pub, from the ones which had been done up to represent 'ye olde englishe pub', to pubs with huge satellite TVs so that no Englishman would have to live without *Match of the Day* while they were on holiday. At one particular bar, they were showing a repeat of the controversial Evander Holyfield vs Mike Tyson fight, and the gathered throng of English football supporters, who had had more than enough to drink, were dancing the can-can and shouting at Tyson on the screen:

"Bite his fucking ear off,
Bite his fucking ear off,
Na-na-na-na, Na-na-na-na."

Some of the pubs were really no more than discos with live entertainment in the form of a PA or band, but whatever type of music you were into, there was a pub which catered to your taste. There was a rock 'n' roll pub with a Status Quo 'tribute' band, karaoke clubs with Gary Glitter lookalikes, and several jazz pubs, too.

To appease the tourists, most of the black artists working the Playa de Las Americas strip posed as 'ex-Drifters', 'ex-Supremes', 'ex-Temptations, despite not looking anything like anybody who had ever been a member of those legendary groups. These phony 'Motown' artists often performed five or six different gigs a night each.

It didn't take Johnny long to notice that there wasn't much unity amongst the few black folk on the island. He soon gave up hailing the African American tourists he encountered on the promenade, as their reaction to seeing his dreadlocked mane was to clutch their handbags tighter. As if that wasn't bad enough, the four friends ended up cradling double screwdrivers in a dimly-lit bar, where the highest paid black entertainer on the island was doing his light entertainment set and making jokes about the Senegalese street traders who hawked their leather goods and cheap watches on every other street corner. "Anyone want to buy a belt?" the entertainer winked at his mainly white audience, as if to say, any black man you meet on this island apart from me is an illegal street trader selling leather goods.

There were nightclubs with names such as Billion Dollar Babes, Copacabana and La Luz, where Essex girls dressed up like tarts with deliberately cheap make-up and wearing white stilettoes, pink glossy lipstick — the kind that smudges when snogged — and white miniskirts... It all seemed somehow so unreal.

The four south Londoners ended up for a while at a club/pub called Soul Train. It was now midnight and the place had just started to get busy, which was just as well because Linvall, Gussie and Johnny wanted to start checking the talent immediately.

Where women were concerned, Gussie was the type of guy who liked to flash his money about and, before very long, he was buying out the Soul Train bar and working undercover as the nephew of the King of Saudi Arabia. It seemed to do the trick, as six or seven women had their arms around him and were competing with each other to hug him up and love him up. That is until his money ran out and they followed it hurriedly.

Yes, thought Linvall, with a lick of his lips as he admired the excess amount of girls in the area, this is my type of club. The only drawback was that Soul Train needed someone like Mistri to come over and show them what 'up to date' means. The club's deejay was about twelve months behind with his musical selection and was playing tunes that were released from time and, even then, he would play an old tune three times in one night. The music was seriously wack.

Johnny's thoughts exactly. As far as he was concerned, what Soul Train needed was a dread at the controls and if he wasn't too busy chirpsing he would have stormed the deejay booth.

Johnny's favourite chat-up line in Soul Train was: "Gal pickney, you know why dem call Jamaica 'Land of Wood'? Well, let me put it this way, ship haffe sail over the ocean, boat haffe sail over the sea, if yuh lucky, gal, you'll sail under me. You on the bottom an' me deh 'pon top. That's why they call Jamaica..."

He tried this approach several times, bafflingly without success.

Linvall, who fancied himself as Mr Sex and Soul, preferred to use the line: "Ladeez, you ever had a guy who could satisfy you both all night long?"

The two girls kissed their teeth at him. "Whatever happened to 'Hello, good evening, how are you'?" one of them wondered.

Johnny was in no doubt that one of two Brazilian girls that he was chirpsing was R.A.W. (Ready and Waiting). She clearly wanted to be involved in some oral copulation. Even now she was probably thinking that if she gave the lick she might get the stick, Johnny reasoned with himself. However, he made the mistake of asking Beres to occupy her less attractive friend in conversation while he went to work on sorting out a good grind with the criss one. Beres was the last man to rely on when it came to chirpsing. Because he was the kind of guy whose chat-up line might be, "I know this sounds like a cliché, but do you come here often?" Instead of being like most men and doing a 'Barry White': "Baby, did anyone tell you your eyes are like the velvet of the midnight sky?"

Whatever it was that Beres was saying to the less attractive Brazilian girl it seemed to be irritating her, because she simply ignored him and, with her arms folded, she chewed rapidly on a stick of gum.

Yes, Johnny was thinking, this criss Brazilian gal is definitely ready for the stick. He could just feel it in his bones. In fact, he was so sure that there was going to be some loud moaning and groaning in Las Vinas tonight, that he asked Linvall if he could lend him five or six condoms for the night.

"Johnny, do I look like a chemist to you?" Linvall replied bitterly. Spar or no spar, as far as he was concerned, if he wasn't getting any poom-poom tonight, he definitely wasn't going to be aiding and abetting anyone else.

By this time, the less attractive Brazilian girl had had enough of Beres rabbiting on about his eight-year-old daughter back in England, and indicated to her friend in no uncertain terms that they should leave. Alone. The criss Brazilian girl had little choice. Shrugging her shoulders in resignation, she pecked Johnny on the cheek and said that maybe she'd see him again sometime.

Johnny turned to Beres with daggers in his eyes. He felt like slapping him. "Man, you're sabotaging my chances," he hissed.

41

Patrick Augustus

From Soul Train, they moved on to a Caribbean theme restaurant/pub called Treasure Island, where the now unsober Gussie amused himself on the mini-golf course. Treasure Island charged twenty pounds to get in but you could drink as much cheap plonk as you wanted . As a result, there were some randy women in there who were determined not to leave until the last bottle of wine on the premises had been consumed.

The resident band at Treasure Island was a four-piece calypso outfit called Panache, which consisted of two upfront steel pan players, a bass guitarist and a drummer, playing old time tunes like *Linstead Market, Yellow Bird, Rivers of Babylon* and *I Can See Clearly Now,* for the tourists. The band were so good at their job that they even succeeded in getting a whole bunch of old folks who hadn't shaken a leg in years to do the 'okey-cokey' calypso style.

Johnny and his friends felt great. It was nice to just kick back and relax, far from the troubles of life. That's what they had come to Tenerife for. They wanted to be a million miles away from all the distress that waited for them back in London.

"Me recognize dat yout' deh," Johnny pointed to the tall dark-skinned rastaman with the long locks on the lead pan.

When the group came off stage at the end of their set, Johnny called the youth over. The pan player obliged and approached their table in that shoulders-back, light-on-the-toes way people have when they run miles every morning, lift weights, don't eat red meat and snack on fat-free crisps.

"Me know you, y'know," Johnny said.

The tall dreadlocks nodded. "Seeeeeen."

"So where me know you from? You live ah Brixton?"

"Yes man, born and grow, y'know. To be honest, you probably know me as an author. I wrote a book called *Baby Father.*"

"Fe true? Bumboclaat!" Johnny laughed. "Ah you named Patrick Augustus? Yes my yout', touch me." Johnny offered his clenched fist to Patrick. Patrick touched it with his own clenched fist. "Siddung, my yout'. You fe drink one drink with me an' my idren dem."

Patrick thanked him for the invitation and sat down. After being introduced to everyone, he admitted that they didn't get too many black tourists coming to Treasure Island and that he always made sure he took time out to reason with them whenever they came.

"The food here's not all that though," he warned. "You're better off holding a bag of chips. Tene-grief have 'nuff fish and chip shops. Wait a minute..." Patrick paused, the realization dawning on him. "Wasn't it you guys who were on the *Janet Sinclair Show* recently? We get it over here on satellite. Rahtid, it was you, wasn't it? Your women went in front of the cameras and gave you the living distress. Bwoy, I don't know how you guys handled it. If my woman put me to shame like that on TV it would have been 'war inna babylon'."

The four friends shuffled around uneasily in their seats. The last thing they wanted to discuss at this moment was their appearance on the talk show. Johnny changed the subject quickly.

"So, Patrick, what you doing out here? I thought you were a top notch author. What you doing playing steel pans in Tenerife?"

"Me is a musician, y'know, star. In fact, I had hit records long before I started writing books. Remember the tune *Horse Move* by Horseman? Ah my tune dat, star. Went to number one inna the hit parade. Ah no not'n."

"You know, me just love your books," Johnny said.

"Me too," agreed Linvall.

"That makes three of us," said a tipsy Gussie.

Beres didn't quite agree.

"I think your books give a false impression that all black men are irresponsible absent fathers," he said stiffly. "And, quite frankly, that's not true. Some of us try and do the right thing. Some of us want to be there one hundred percent for our partners and our children."

Trust Beres to cold up the vibes. Johnny groaned.

"You're missing the point of the books," Johnny said. "My man's books are supposed to give you one and two joke. Ah dat him ah deal with. Strictly entertainment business. No need to take it too seriously. Skeen?"

"To be honest I read those *Baby Father* books to get a lot of information and advice on how to outsmart your woman," Linvall chirped in. "I can tell you, there's been one or two times when I've been in a tricky situation, even caught red-handed on the job, and I've got out of the situation by taking one or two moves out of the *Baby Father* books."

"Yes man, I agree completely," Johnny added. "Especially that part in the first *Baby Father* book, where you're talking about polygamy an' saying that polygamy is the only way many of the excess amount of single black women out there in the community are going to get some loving nowadays. When I showed my women dem that, none of them could argue with it. They all had to admit that if they didn't have a man, they would rather be in the situation where they had a man part-time an' shared him amongst several other women, than not have a man at all."

Beres didn't buy that argument at all. "Talk like that is negative. We should be building up the community, and the only way we can do that is by going *black* to basics — *black* to life, *black* to one woman and one man and *black* to the family which is at the centre of everything. When the family is united and strong, the community prospers. When it's destroyed by wanton promiscuity we suffer. Don't you think there's enough unofficial polygamy out there already without you needing to encourage more?"

"Look, Beres, in certain ways I agree with you, I was even going to get married because of it," Johnny reminded his friend with a long sigh. "I was prepared to overlook all my past ways an' set up as an item with Lesley, just because I thought it was the right thing to do. Just to give my youths some guidance. But when I start checking my Bible now, I could see that all ah them great men like Solomon and King David were polygamous. Then I get to understand why dem man deh were so wise…"

"That's the problem with your reasoning, "Beres countered, "the Bible makes it perfectly clear that God desires men and women to come together, fall in love,

Patrick Augustus

be faithful to one another, marry and raise children — in that order. If you were living in the days of old and your name was King Solomon or King David, it might have been okay to be polygamous. But this is the nineties, Johnny. We're moving into the twenty-first century and you live in south London where it's hard enough bringing up one family without trying to stretch your resources even more by having concubines. I hear that if you go and live in Tanzania they will accommodate you and your lifestyle, but not in the society we live in. All the sadness, heartache and pain that kind of fatherhood brings is a world away from the happiness and contentment God desires men and women to experience in their partnerships with one another. Why are you unable to be content with one woman? Why can't you be faithful? I have fallen in love with two women at the same time before and wanted to have them both, but I realized it couldn't work and I had to make a choice... It's that simple. The message of the Bible seems clear — don't be greedy."

"*Me* greedy? No sah. You can tell that to the ladies. 'Cause when I was a teenager, I wasn't interested in any women. They came to me. I was happy studying, practicing a little football every now an' then an' playing on the pinball machine. I didn't even want any women around me. As far as I was concerned, they were interfering nuisances. But then three girls wanted to go out with me at the same time. You hear dat? I didn't want to go out with them, they wanted to go out with me. An' each one ah dem put a lot of pressure on me, I couldn't decide which one to go out with. Finally,

46

I decided 'Chuh, mek me go out with all ah dem'. An' guess what, they all agreed to share me. That's how I changed from not wanting women, to wanting too many…"

"So Johnny, are you saying you haven't been a bad father?"

"*Me?* No, me no bad father."

"You don't think that having children all over the place is being a bad father?"

Johnny hesitated, unsure of where Beres was going with this argument.

"Yes or no?" Beres insisted. "Answer that."

"No! No! No!!"

"So tell me, Johnny, how do you manage to feed all your children?" Beres asked. It was a question he had been meaning to ask for years.

"Well, love is all I have so love is all I bring…"

"You see what I mean? Children need cash, Johnny. Love doesn't pay their food, clothing and shelter," Beres said. "I've known you from time, Johnny, and I've studied you in your dealings with all your women and, frankly, I've had to come to the conclusion that it's a disease with you. That you're just addicted to sex. I bet you, you couldn't last one whole week of celibacy."

"Put it this way, I'd never say no. Even if I met a woman and she was feeling a bit randy and I wasn't. Men need to get fresh oats regularly. An' I'm sorry, one woman can't give me that."

"I agree with Johnny," said Linvall. "You never hear a man say 'no' to sex, whereas the other way round, women are more likely to say 'not tonight, Joe'. That's the problem with being in a monogamous relationship. What can you do if your woman keeps saying 'no'? Women know the power they've got over us. They know that we're slaves to sex. Some women use this power a manipulative way — 'Be a good boy and you'll get what you want'. And even if I'm getting sex regularly from my woman, ideally I would still like more sexual partners. In an ideal world you'd be able to meet someone at a bus stop, go for a drink, take them home and bonk their brains out, and then go home to your girlfriend for dinner."

"More women doesn't solve the problem though, does it?" Beres asked. "The more women you have, the more you want. And even when you're not getting it, you spend your time entertaining fantasies about women with whom you have not yet had a sexual relationship. Think about the amount of time you spend on that, if you used that time constructively, you'd be richer than the whole lot of us put together."

Johnny thought about it for a moment, Beres had a point. But realistically, that wasn't feasible. He didn't know one man who put personal wealth and reputation before the wickedest slam.

"Every man fantasizes about having sex with a woman he's never had sex with — don't they?" Linvall asked.

"I don't." said Beres stiffly.

"Well I can't stop doing it. I only have to see a woman — any woman — and my imagination starts thinking about a quick bonk in the back seat of my car."

"That doesn't sound too romantic to me," Beres

sneered.

"It's not supposed to be romantic. I'm not a romantic and I'm proud of that. Romance is for fools and, anyway, it never lasts. Once you got what you're after, what's the point of being lovey dovey? Unless you've done something wrong and you think, jeez, I better pop down to Safeway for a bag of flowers and a box of chocolates."

"Don't you lose respect for a woman who would sleep with you on the first date?" Beres asked.

"Nah man," Johnny said decisively. "Me only lose respect if she's not giving up the t'ings like she's supposed to."

"You guys are wasting your lives," Beres pointed out. "It's only sex. Sex with one woman is the same as the next."

That point made both Linvall and Johnny stop a while and think. Linvall had no choice but to fantasize about other women, considering the current rationing of his sex life. Johnny, on the other hand, was wondering whether he hadn't had more sex in his life than one man should reasonably expect to have. Beres definitely had a point, he had been overdosing on it, but what could he do, he was hooked.

"So, Johnny, back to my point," Beres continued, "I bet you couldn't live without sex for the next seven days."

"I bet you I could," said Johnny. It was his mind doing the bravado talking, not his head.

"How much do you want to bet?"

"Here's the two grand I made from the sales of the

Bibles."

Johnny pulled out a wad of crisp twenty pound notes
from his back pocket and dropped it on the table.

"You're on," said Beres without hesitation.

They shook hands on the matter. Beres smiled a
satisfied smile and leaned back in his chair.

"I'm going to enjoy watching you trying to survive
throughout this holiday without sex," he told Johnny.

"Johnny, you're mad," Linvall said, shaking his
head. "I would never have made a bet like that, not on
this holiday."

It was only then that it started to sink into Johnny's
common sense. He had agreed that, on this Tenerife
holiday where women were virtually thrusting their
hips into your face, he would resist any feminine
charms. He decided to amend the bet slightly.

"Well, I'm only going to go without penetrative sex.
I mean, I can still chirps women, and I can still go to bed
with them, just not end up doing anything. You get
me?"

Beres thought about this for a moment. Still
confident that Johnny could not survive without a full
bag of oats, he agreed to the amendment.

If he was honest with himself, Beres would admit
that he was not himself immune to the many charms of
women, but he was not prepared to jeopardize a nuclear
relationship, with mother, father and children all living
under the same roof, for the sake of one night of
passion. If he could get away with it, fair enough, but it
wasn't worth getting caught for. He could admit that to
himself but he wouldn't admit it to Johnny. Johnny

needed all the help he could get to get over this destructive addiction and Beres was not about to give him ammunition to defend his lifestyle with. That's what spars were for — to keep each other on the straight and narrow and get the best out of life. Nor would Beres reveal to Johnny that, secretly, he felt that there was no harm in fantasizing about other women — being mentally unfaithful. For all Beres knew, women everywhere did the same. The last thing that he certainly wasn't going to admit to Johnny under the circumstances, was that he himself had brought a packet of condoms on this trip, just in case... After all, he was effectively estranged from his partner, wasn't he?

"Where's my yout' gone?" Johnny asked, suddenly looking up. They had been talking between them for almost an hour and had forgotten all about Patrick Augustus. He seemed to have vanished completely.

From Treasure Island, Johnny, Linvall, Beres and Gussie staggered to Café Hedonist, where only a handful of late night drinkers remained, still unwilling to return to their hotel rooms. The four south Londoners had hardly been in the bar a few minutes when an attractive Spanish woman who had been sitting by herself, quietly getting drunk in a corner, came over and pulled Gussie up to dance. He was only too happy to oblige and, alone on the dance floor, they got down with some dirty dancing under the heavy influence of alcohol. They didn't need any music, either. It got so dirty, in fact, that an innocent bypasser looking in through the window might have been forgiven for thinking that a live sex show was taking place.

His friends applauded as Gussie taught the girl the 'cock up your batty' dance he was inclined to do with women when he was drunk.

The young Spanish waiter who came over to the table to take their orders was not amused by Gussie's antics however. Steam started coming out of his ears and fumes out of his nostrils as he watched Gussie on the dance floor teaching the girl the 'get down on the lollipop' dance.

"Hey," he told the three seated friends, "tell your friend — no dance wiz my woman," the waiter told them with a heavy accent. "That iss my kurlfriend."

"Hey bwoy, tell her yourself, man," Johnny replied. "Anyway, she don't look like your girlfriend to me." He kissed his teeth. "Chuh man, just get us our beers, and make it snappy. 'Bout tell Gussie dis an' dat... Chuh man, wha' do you?"

The waiter looked at them vengefully and went to get the drinks.

If Johnny hadn't been so tipsy already, he would have remembered, from going to Chinese restaurants in London, that you don't want to abuse the waiters before they bring you your order. At one Chinese restaurant, where he had come into an altercation with one of the waiters, he had ended up crunching on a toenail served with his vegetarian fried rice.

This waiter was a hardcore raver in his other life, and never went anywhere without a few hallucinogenic controlled substances in his possession. He decided to teach these black Englishmen a lesson.

Having drunk a couple more pints of beer each, the

four friends were feeling… Well, they weren't quite sure how they were feeling. Only Linvall had ever felt this way before, but that was at a rave on a Saturday night. It couldn't possible be…

It was so late, they could almost call it early and the four friends decided to make their way back home. The drunken Spanish woman had suddenly remembered that her boyfriend was taking her home and Gussie was too 'trippy' to make anything of it. He just needed to visit the 'Gents' before they departed. His friends watched Gussie stagger away.

The toilet was remarkably clean and, despite its lack of pissoires, Gussie was only too grateful to be able to relieve himself in a toilet that didn't smell of camel breath. He let out a satisfied sigh as a hot stream of dark yellow urine flowed out and, despite himself, let out a ripping fart. It was at that moment that the person occupying the next cubicle came out and saw Gussie through the open door to his cubicle. She let out a scream. It was only as he was being dragged out of the toilet by one of the bouncers in the club that Gussie noticed that the sign on the door said 'Ladies'.

As the four friends made their way home from Club Hedonism, their worlds started spinning around. Johnny didn't want to admit it, in case he sounded as if he couldn't take his drink, but he wasn't feeling too good. Neither was Beres. Linvall was enjoying the buzz that he was getting and was considering taking a couple of crates of that beer back home to London with him. Gussie had been unsober so long, that he didn't feel any difference.

Patrick Augustus

The streets were almost empty, most of the tourists having gone to their beds. Only the most hardcore stragglers were still out looking for a final drink or someone to take home with them. Several others were making a public display of how much vomit they could bring up in one go. The two girls outside the ice cream stall thought their luck had come in when they saw the four well-dressed black men passing through.

"Oi, my mate wants to snog you," one of them called out.

Johnny was the first to respond. "Dat can't run, you know," he told the girl in no uncertain terms. "Dat can't work t'raasclaat."

"Go on, just a little snog, she really likes you."

"I tell you what," he said, "I really like the way you're licking that ice cream. I'd like you to lick my balls like that. By the way, I'm a battytician so, while you're licking my balls, I'll examine your posterior and tell you whether it looks enormous in those jeans."

Johnny couldn't explain his strange behaviour. He had never spoken to a woman quite that explicitly before. But he couldn't stop himself.

One of the girls looked like she was definitely up for the idea, but her friend pulled her away in a fit of giggles.

It was one of those sultry nights which was made for bonking. Back at Las Vinas, everybody in the compound seemed to be bonking the night away, everybody that is except Beres, Linvall, Johnny and Gussie. All they could hear as they made their way across the landscaped gardens to their chalet was excessively loud moaning

54

and groaning from the other tourist chalets as grinding and climaxing mixed together in a cacophony of lovemaking sounds. From inside their chalet, the four friends could hear a cuckolded boyfriend trying to get back into the flat. "Open up," he kept calling out angrily, while everybody in the whole compound could hear quite clearly that his girlfriend was inside grinding somebody else.

Uhhhhhhhhhn... unnn-unh-unhhhhh... Unnnnnnnnh, unnnnnh-hunnnnn...

The sounds floated out of the open first floor window and out into the cool summer night, it made its way around the leafy compound, rattling the windows of every chalet as it went along.

Unnnnnnnhhhhh-unnnnnnnnn-mmmmmmmmm, unnnnnnnh, unnnnnnh-unnnnh...

There was nothing quite like the sensual sound of a woman sighing with sheer sweet pleasure as she engaged in a spot of illicit sex while her partner was locked outside unable to get in. It was a sound that sounded like it came floating down from the heavens and every now and then there would be a rapid, staccato cry of ecstacy.

Las Vinas was certainly a horny little place.

Johnny had never had an LSD trip before, but he imagined that it must feel something like he felt now. He couldn't believe how everything seemed to be going in slow motion. He couldn't explain why his head was buzzing, but the last thing he wanted to do was go to bed. Beres felt the same way, too. Gussie was both drunk and buzzing. He didn't feel like throwing up any more, all he wanted now was a game of dominoes. Well, it wasn't so much a proposal as a challenge.

"You remember that time I gave you that six-nil," he teased Johnny.

"You never give ME no six-nil," Johnny dismissed him with a wave of his hand. However 'trippy' he felt, he was sober enough to defend his honour at the domino table.

"Yes six-nil, man. I tell a lie, I tell a lie. It was six-nil twice. Most definitely. Beres was a witness, isn't that right, B?"

Beres smiled. Yes, that was a memorable game. At the time, Johnny got really under the collar about being thrashed at the game he claimed to be a master of by a novice such as Gussie.

Johnny's memory was selective at the best of times.

"When you speak to me concerning dominoes, you know seh you haffe speak with your head bowed, and address me as 'sir', don't? 'Cause I am an *h*expert in the field of dominoes."

"Yeah, yeah, yeah. I beat you easy, you're not the 'master' you're the apprentice. Most definitely. Isn't that so, prento?" Gussie teased.

The gauntlet had been thrown down. Johnny told Gussie loudly about exactly what kind of beating he was going to have to endure. Johnny ran upstairs to pull the dominoes out of his luggage for the first time on this holiday. He descended like a gunslinger from the wild west walking into the saloon for the big showdown, his head buzzing furiously. Though he had never taken speed before, Gussie figured that this must be what it's like.

Uhhhhhhhhhn... unnn-unh-unhhhhh... Unnnnnnnnnh, unnnnnh-hunnnnn... Unnnnnhhhhm.

That sound again.

The four friends shifted uneasily. One by one they went to the glass patio door and looked out. They knew exactly which apartment it was coming from.

Uhhhhhhhhhn... unnn-unh-unhhhhh... Unnnnnnnnnh, unnnnnh-hunnnnn... Unnnnnhhhhm.

They looked up to the first floor window in the moonlight shadow and saw the silhouette of a pair of legs pointing to the ceiling, and each of them wondered why it wasn't him in there, thrilling her to ecstasy.

Uhhhhhhhhhn... unnn-unh-unhhhhh... Unnnnnnnnnh, unnnnnh-hunnnnn... Unnnnnhhhhm, she moaned again.

It was the sweetest sound Johnny had ever heard and he longed to be there right now, being hugged and kissed and scratched and bitten and pleading...

Contrary to popular opinion, dominoes is not a kid's game. At least not in the Caribbean community, where the game requires as much testosterone as it does skill. From childhood, Gussie, Beres, Linvall and Johnny were taught that if somebody beat you in dominoes, you beat them back. And if you lost six-nil, you couldn't go home. Those boyhood domino battles became a symbol of manhood, and followed them into adulthood, getting fiercer, louder and more skillful.

Though it is most certainly a man's game, one or two persistent women have tried unsuccessfully to penetrate this final bastion of male domination, but they are as likely to succeed in their efforts as they are to become members of the Lord's Cricket Ground Members Club.

So it was with a lot of shouting and swearing and a lot of slamming the domino cards down hard onto the table, that the first four sets ended 6-5, 6-5, 6-5, 5-6. Johnny claimed that he had been feeling a bit dizzy throughout those games. It was a poor excuse, nevertheless Gussie went upstairs and brought down a bottle of duty free rum to "stop the dizziness". Each man poured out a stiff glass. Then Johnny and his partner Linvall edged forward with a fierce 6-4. Beres and Gussie came back with a 4-6 of their own. To an onlooker, it might have seemed that neither team seemed to take much rejoicing in their meagre victories. Once or twice Johnny had to warn his partner to wake up and pay attention, but apart from that there didn't seem to be much emotion coming from any of them. They were both searching for the elusive six-nil victory that domino players search for in their aim to humiliate their opponents. Without that six-nil, each victory was merely a minor triumph, nothing to shout home about. Six-nil was more like an apocalypse. Six-nil is not so easy though, because an opponent will do anything to avoid such a drubbing.

As both pairs struggled in vain to humiliate their opponents, the game started taking on a distinctively hostile atmosphere, with the players verbally abusing each other. Johnny's frustration had something to do with the buzz in his head. He so wanted to give Gussie a six-nil, that Linvall's every mistake caused his high blood pressure to rise.

"Ah why de bumboclaat you ah put down the double-six when you can see clearly I couldn't play?!" he exploded when they had been close (but not close enough) with a six-one victory. "Did you never learn to read when you were at school? So how come you can't read the cards? It's all that masturbating you've been doing, just because your commanding wife's giving you a recession, isn't it?"

Gussie poured himself another glass of rum and laughed.

"You see, Johnny, me and Beres have just been letting you pick up a few games, but now it's time to get your ass most definitely burned and buried proper."

Johnny poured himself a tumbler full of rum and cursed Gussie. He suggested that to make things more interesting that they should place a £5 bet on the outcome of each game. The others agreed.

Johnny and Linvall lost the next game. In fact they lost four games in a row. They were twenty pounds down and, this time, Johnny's venom turned to Beres, who he accused of not playing the game by the official (Jamaican) rules.

"You see, that's why I don't like playing dominoes with a Bajan. You Bajans have your lickle small island ways of playing domino. Small island, small willy, that's what I say."

Johnny didn't know what made him cuss his friend in such a way, it was like he was no longer in control of his actions. It felt like he had been smoking skunk weed all night long and was now totally off his head. Still, Gussie and Linvall found it amusing and they started laughing hysterically at Beres for they, like Johnny, were both Jamaicans.

Beres didn't take too kindly to this slight on his national heritage. He was from Barbados, and proud of it. He had never once smoked a spliff before, let alone ingest any other form of controlled substance. He couldn't understand how a few drinks could have made him feel like he was floating on a natural high. He felt like he wanted to throw all his clothes off and streak down to the beach for a midnight swim.

"Trust you Jamaicans to lower the tone of the conversation," he retorted. "Don't worry about the size of my sexual organ. Just because I don't need to hug it all the time like you, doesn't mean that my sexuality is vulnerable. In fact, when it comes to my sexual performance *and* penis size, to be honest I have always received flattering comments on both scores. However, knowing that women generally tend to flatter, I take this with a pinch of salt."

Johnny laughed. Beres was usually 'Mr Discreet' when it came to discussing matters of a sexual nature. It was most unusual to hear him discussing his sexual ability so openly. But Johnny couldn't let him get away with the self-praise.

"That's not what I heard. I heard you were one ah dem guys who only makes love once a week an', even then, only in the missionary position. An' I heard that your willy was no bigger than my lickle finger."

"Put your money where your mouth is," Beres said, with a determined look. "Come on. You think you're the greatest — prove it."

"What makes you think you're qualified to test I and I?" Johnny retorted. The challenge took him by surprise. Cockiness never did suit Beres. On the other hand, it did suit him: "Me will run a woman up the wall with my boss cock. Trust me."

How did Beres intend to prove otherwise, except by exposing himself? It was one thing to share a chalet with other men, or to ask a man if your posterior protruded excessively in your attire, but the rules amongst spars was that you kept your private parts to yourself and you always made sure that you avoided looking at your friend's tackle even if the bath towel fell from around his waist. In circumstances like that you fixed your gaze at a spot on the wall behind him, to ensure that there was no misunderstanding. Every man has a penis hang up, and the last thing you need is to be caught up in the next man's. But Beres was determined to prove the point there and then, on the living room table.

"Well, there's no need…" Johnny began.

"No excuses," Beres insisted. "I'm tired of hearing all these jibes from you Jamaicans about how small a Bajan man's manhood is. Let's settle it now and for all. A hundred quid says that I've got the biggest penis here."

That wasn't just a challenge to Johnny, but to Linvall and Gussie also. Their heads were buzzing too much to resist and, for now, the domino game was all but forgotten about. Each man ran upstairs to his bedroom to pull out a hundred pounds in travellers cheques.

They sat there, all four of them, around the pile of traveller's cheques on the living room table, each man waiting for the other to pull out his piece. Nobody wanted to be first. So they pulled straws. Gussie pulled the shortest straw.

A little reluctantly, he pulled down his zip and revealed a penis of average size.

Johnny was next. Confidently, he whipped out his golden pistol and proudly displayed why women had raved about it ever since he was a schoolboy.

Linvall gasped.

Beres was next. He eased down his zipper and with his left hand started pulling out his piece, and just kept on pulling... It was absolutely enormous. The longest, thickest beast they had ever seen. Gussie knew for sure that he was most definitely tripping on a hallucinatory drug. He closed his eyes and shook his head. Then he opened his eyes again, but Beres' monster was still there staring him in the face threateningly.

Linvall gasped again.

All Johnny could say was "bumbo-CLAAT!" That's how small Beres' penis made his own look.

Linvall didn't want to play any more, but the others insisted. They had exposed themselves and Linvall had to do the same.

When he finally summed up the courage, Linvall drew his zip down very slowly. The others waited. And waited...

Then suddenly, Linvall let out a scream.

"Help! Damn! Shit! It's shrunk. My dick's shrunk. I swear to God, it's shrunk... This morning, it was the size of Beres'. I swear! Shit..."

Johnny kissed his teeth. "This is not a boast-to-your-friends-down-the-lane t'ing, y'know." How could a man with buck teeth lie so bad, he wondered. "Anyway," he said to Beres as he handed him his traveller's cheques, "most women I've known say it's not the size but what you do with it that counts."

The sharp knocking on the patio doors caught them all by surprise. They turned to see a smiling black face peering through the glass. Each man took cover as quickly as he could. But it was too late. She had seen everything there was to see.

Having pulled up his zip, Johnny bashfully opened the patio door.

"I'm sorry to disturb you…" she began, the smile on her face widening all the time as she looked over Johnny's shoulder at Beres. "I'm from next door. I heard through the walls that you were still up. We're two sistas from London and we can't get to sleep. Our plumbing needs attending to…"

"Don't worry about dat one bit," said Johnny bigging up his chest, "I'll come over and sort you out."

The woman looked Johnny up and down woefully. "I think it's too big a job for you. But I think *you* can handle it," she pointed at Beres.

Ever the gentleman, Beres was quick to offer his services and, without further ado, followed the woman next door.

Johnny, Gussie and Linvall were left with their mouths open wide and feeling very horny the rest of the night.

It was only the first night, the holiday was far from over. Or in Johnny's words as he tried to put a brave face on things: "Dis nuh finish, it nuh finish…"

YAGGA-YAGGA

Johnny's dream was really a nightmare. There he is, old and destitute and living in the gutter outside the Dorchester Hotel on Park Lane. It is a grey Monday morning and even the grandness of the hotel does little to lighten the winter morning blues. The door man, behind a red, raw nose and goose pimples, shrugs off his obvious discomfort and greets guests with a Hollywood smile. Beaverish hotel staff attend to the chaos outside whilst visitors with weekend hangovers hibernate in their rooms. Suddenly the clouds part and the sun begins to shine as a Rolls Royce pulls up and out of it step his many children looking like a million dollars, dripping huge diamonds on their fingers and gold everywhere. He calls out his daughter's name. She turns around and looks on the old beggar. "Damn, I thought you had croaked," she says. "I'm in an awful hurry. See you around some time."

But Johnny won't let go of her ankle.

"I did my part to bring you into this world," he pleads with her. "Please, don't treat me like a dog. All I need is some loose change for a cup of tea. You look like you've got the money. Are you married to some rich man? Do I have any grandchildren?"

But his daughter Winnie simply sneers. "I made it on

my own, no thanks to you," she says. "Read about me in the Sunday Times 'rich list', it will tell you where I made my money and how. I'm one of the richest women in the country, and you'll never get a penny from me."

"Please don't leave me here in the gutter, I'm your flesh an' blood... You're my seed..."

"Yeah right, rejuvenating your balls was the only thing you were ever good at," Winnie concludes before kicking him to the curb.

Johnny woke up from his nightmare unsure of the unfamiliar surroundings. It took him a moment or two to distinguish dream from reality. Yes, he really was in Tenerife, on holiday with his closest spars. But what of last night? Had that all been a dream? Had they really met *Baby Father* author Patrick Augustus in a bar? That seemed unlikely. More importantly, what of Beres, had he really managed to get off with the girl next door? That seemed unlikely, too. Not to talk of Beres winning the 'dickie inspection'. No, he must have been dreaming, either that or he must have been tripping. The only way you could get four black men to pull out their dicks like that would be if they were totally smashed out of their skulls on some hallucinatory chemical drugs. No, he concluded, he must have been dreaming.

He got up and went downstairs. Linvall and Gussie were already up and playing a sedate game of dominoes on the patio. Beres was nowhere to be seen.

"He's probably still next door giving that bird a good banging I imagine," said Linvall.

So it was true? Johnny couldn't believe it. "Just

because he's got a big dick!"

After a long discussion about how women were penis-fixated, the three men decided to go down to the beach and check the talent out. They left a note for Beres before they left, informing him of when they would be back.

Dressed in beach shorts and t-shirts, the dreadlocks, the funki dred and the baldhead (in the xtra-xtra-xtra large outfit to hide the paunch that was bulging before him), went out in the blazing midday sun amongst all the other tourists and wandered down to the Playa de Las Americas promenade.

As usual, the promenade was full of English tourists spending their money in the pubs and restaurants. Down on the beach, the topless bathing was in full swing despite the signs declaring that it was strictly forbidden. The three friends managed to pick a good spot to await any 'made in the shade' ladies who might be coming their way.

"Can you believe that that wotless Beres, who don't really know how to handle a gal proper, could get off with such a criss woman?" Johnny asked.

"Beats me," Gussie agreed, his well-oiled head glistening in the sun.

"I was up all night thinking about him giving her the bedwork..."

"Me too," said Gussie.

"That makes three of us," Linvall concurred.

Johnny laughed.

"Anyway, I hear that 'big' boys can't keep it up very long, on account of all that weight they're carrying..."

Baby Father 3: *Does my batty look big in this?*

Linvall's thoughts wandered off as he watched the waves lapping up the sand. He was definitely looking forward to getting off the starting mark and checking some girls, but at the same time he was terrified about getting home and his woman finding out about it. He didn't know how she would, he just knew that she would, that's the kind of woman Marcia was. He had even brought an idiot-proof instamatic camera down to the beach and had taken photos of trees along the promenade, taking good care to make sure that there were no scantily-clad women in view, so that when Marcia inspected the photographic evidence on his return to London she would get the impression that they had spent their holiday on a nature reserve or something. Yeah, *right!* She had him under such heavy manners, and she was so cunning and sly about these things, that there was no knowing what she would pick up on, that would give the game away. Then off course his goose would have been well and truly cooked.

In all this time that he and his wife had been back together again Linvall had been dreaming of when he would finally get the opportunity to check other women en masse again, he had been scheming and working it out for nearly a year now. He knew exactly what he would do when he got the chance. There wouldn't be any foreplay — hell no. In fact, he didn't care whether the woman enjoyed it or not. What he needed more than anything was to meet a woman who was willing to simply bonk his brains out.

The last thing Johnny needed in his life was a woman who could bonk his brains out. He had had plenty of

Patrick Augustus

those already. That kind of loving was what got him into this problem in the first place. He was now paying his dues, paying for all those years of recklessness. He tried to imagine how wonderful life would have been if he hadn't been strapped down with kids and three baby mothers. How could he not have understood that every child would bring with it a lifetime of problems, not to talk of commitments?

When he thought about it, women who could bonk his brains out had also lost him a whole heap of money over the years. Hard cash. He felt used and abused, but knew that if he bumped into a woman who could bonk his brains out on this trip, he would lose even more money to Beres in a bet that he now realized was a lose-lose situation. He must have been crazy to bet when, deep inside, he knew himself well enough to know that he couldn't resist a woman who could potentially bonk his brains out. He just couldn't and wouldn't.

Sitting in the sun on a beach doing absolutely nothing but taking in the seductive scenery was the kind of life Johnny could get used to. Tenerife was like paradise compared to the misery he had waiting for him back home in London. If only he could live out here permanently… It would be cool for the weather, women and everything else. But that was just a pipedream. The reality was, he only had six more days in Tenerife and then he had to go back home to four kids and three angry baby mothers. He wasn't relishing having to face that kind of music.

All this thinking about home and his problems was taking a lot of fun out of Johnny's holiday. The only

68

thing that could succeed in getting his mind off all this woe was, once again, a woman who could bonk his brains out.

"So how are you going to last seven days without checking any of the beautiful women out here?" Linvall asked suddenly.

Johnny shrugged his shoulders.

"Beautiful or not, there's always a woman out there who will tempt a man. It all depends on the man whether or not he will allow himself to be tempted and how strong he is otherwise. Anyway, Beres is going to have catch me red-handed first." He laughed. "He must think I'm some kind of fool if he expects me to come all the way out here to Tenerife with all this topless sunbathing, and not end up with some criss sista inna me bed."

What Johnny decided, was up to him. Gussie had every intention of enjoying himself to the max now that he had, somehow, survived certain disaster on the journey here. Enjoying himself to the max meant getting as much sex as he could. Going off on holiday with your best friends was nice, but they were guys. He needed a woman on heat. He glanced around the beach and took in a couple of eyefuls of the bathing beauties, especially the topless ones. He turned his shaven head this way and that, trying to keep his mind off the fact that he would soon be the father of twins.

It had always been his dream to have children, that dream was now being realized and at the same time being taken away from him. He should never have signed that surrogate father contract which relinquished any rights towards his kids. How was he going to live with the fact that he had two children out there that didn't belong to him?

"Hello baby," Gussie called out to a particularly attractive bronzed beauty walking barefoot on the sand.

"Goodbye!" she called back.

"Yeah, right," Gussie replied. "I bet we'll be making love by the end of the week."

"Sweetheart, I wouldn't give you the time of the day to find out what I've got," the girl called back.

Feeling chastised, and determined not to let her have the last word, Gussie shouted a typically macho male response. The girl didn't hear him, the breeze carried his words out to sea.

Almost absent-mindedly, Johnny began to sing the words of one of his favourite reggae songs:

> *"Fatty boom-boom*
> *Me don't like untidy poom...*
> *So lif' up your skirt*
> *An' mek me inspect*
> *Then when me push in me testament*
> *It won't 'cause a great incident..."*

Then Johnny turned to his friends.

"You know what our problem is, we love poom-poom too much. An' no matter how much we love it, poom-poom never gets stale. I mean, the worst poom-poom is ever going to be in life, is good. Skeen? An' we know seh there's plenty more nice gal out there that we never yet slam. Man an' man is driven by the need to sample every poom-poom in the world... Imagine if we had a little tight poom-poom of our own, in the middle of our hand. Then we wouldn't have to go running to women every time we feel like a little poom. An' they wouldn't be able to enslave us. Women know that they've got the poom-poom an' we ain't got none, so we're slaves to them. At least until they give us a piece. Until then we have to lick batty — literally."

"Speak for yourself man, I don't lick batty," Gussie protested.

"Don't you? I thought every man did," Johnny said.

"Well, it would have to be some pretty special poom-poom for me to lick batty," Linvall added.

"There's no such thing as 'special poom-poom'," Johnny interjected. "Every woman thinks her poom is special. Trust me, they're all the same. If any woman out there thinks their poom-poom is top notch, bring it come, I'd like to give it a second opinion. No, it's not the poom-poom that's important, it's what you can with your rod of correction that's vital. From you have the skill an' you nevah yet spill, you gone clear..."

For a few moments, the three friends were silent, each man lost in his own meditation. Then Johnny came up with a bright idea.

"What men want is what women want... There should be a gentleman's club where, for a small membership fee, you could go along and order a drink and a couple of women to go. Y'know what I mean? A club where you don't have to come up with any more chat-up lines because hostesses will be on call to communicate your sweet nothings to the ladies of your choice. We should start a club of passion where the atmosphere would be very laid-back, not sleazy, where you could turn to the hostess an' say, 'Hey, hostess, I see a woman I would LOVE to meet. That woman over there in the red dress. Tell her that I would like to offer her a glass of champagne and my heart'. An' the hostess would reply, 'That lady over there? Oh yes, sir, a very fine choice. Just a mo…' An' she would go off an' go an' chat-up the women on your behalf."

"Yeah," said Gussie, "then she'd come back and say, 'Sorry, sir, the lady has declined your offer'."

"Then I'd call over to the girl and say, 'Hey gyal! You t'ink you nice? Me wouldn't spit on you if you was on fire! Chuh'!"

Johnny had had enough sun for the day. He was tired and figured on returning to Las Vinas for a siesta. Linvall wanted to stay on the beach for a while longer and take some more photos of trees. Gussie didn't want to stay on the beach, but he wasn't tired either, so while Johnny went back to the chalet, Gussie left Linvall on the beach and went for a stroll in the sun.

Loud classical music was floating out of Beres' bedroom when Johnny returned.

"Ah wha' de bumboclaat?" he cried out as he stepped in. How was he to know it was Beethoven's Fifth.

Beres was lying in his bed looking very content with himself when Johnny burst in. Beethoven was his favourite composer and he often indulged in a symphony to relax.

"So you finally came home," Johnny grinned. "You must have been having some big fun next door."

Beres looked up and smiled. He nodded.

"So is that it?" Johnny said. He wanted to know exactly what happened. "Gimme the details, man."

"Well, there's not much to say," Beres replied.

"For a start you can tell me if you went to bed with her?"

Beres grinned. "I have to admit I did."

"You dirty so and so. Man, you have no shame," Johnny sneered. "You're telling me that I can't control my dick. You're just the same as me."

"I might be the same as you," Beres retorted, "but I am not the one who has made a bet to say that I won't be having sex on this trip."

"Chuh, you're facety," Johnny said. He pressed Beres some more about his night of passion, but Beres kept insisting that to discuss a lady's sexual preferences and ability was conduct unbecoming a gentleman like himself.

Back on the beach, Linvall must have dozed off for twenty minutes or so. When he opened his eyes, he was staring up a beautiful pair of chocolate-coloured legs. A short way away from where he lay on his back on the sand, a beautiful sista had made herself comfortable on a deck chair, taking in the sun.

The temptation was too great for Linvall and he didn't waste any time in getting to his feet and walking over casually.

"Excuse me," he said, looking down at the woman dressed in an itsybitsy teenyweeny white bikini which revealed more chocolate coloured flesh than it covered. And very nice flesh it was, too. But he couldn't see her eyes beneath the sunglasses. He couldn't tell if she was awake or asleep.

"Er, I beg your pardon…" he tried again.

His eye caught sight of the Cartier ladies watch on her left hand. That was £34,000 worth of watch there. He knew, because Gussie had one just like it in his Mighty Diamond shop in Hatton Garden. Linvall's interest grew. Any woman who could spend £34,000 on a watch deserved all the attention she was likely to get.

"It is not my wish to disturb you, but you were like a magnet, pulling me towards you," he said, speeching her like a true playa as he sat down on the sand beside her. "May I compliment you on your exquisite taste, I've been searching all day for a woman wearing a Calvin Klein bikini just like this. You see, I'm a fashion photographer. Linvall Henry. You might have seen my pictures in Cosmo or Vogue."

The next thing Linvall noticed was the huge diamond ring on the woman's wedding finger.

The woman took off her sunglasses to reveal a pair of beautiful almond shaped eyes. She smiled sarcastically.

"You take photos for Cosmo," she said in a soft French accent, "wiz zat little ca-me-ra?"

"That's what I love about women," Linvall said, with a knowing smile. "Think about what the world would be like if we didn't have women to keep us entertained?

Baby Father 3: *Does my batty look big in this?*

Seriously, though, I know a woman who would make a fantastic model when I see one. Women like you are not in abundance and it gives me great pleasure and joy to see you looking like supermodel quality. Of course, you've got a bikini on, albeit an itsybitsy one, however, to give you a full evaluation, I'd have to see what you were like in the nude..."

The woman rolled her eyes. "Why didn't you say zat you wanted to have sex?" she said. "I am also looking for someone to, how you say, bonk my brains out. You have a big cock, yes? *Voulez-vous couchez avec moi, ce soir?*"

Linvall nodded eagerly. He couldn't believe how blunt, direct, and honest this French sista was in seizing the proverbial bull by the horns and taking the direct route. But it didn't bother him. There was nothing Linvall liked better than an impromptu sex session — especially with someone else's wife.

The woman, whose name was Emmanuelle, led Linvall by the hand to her jeep, which was parked a short distance from the beach. She explained that she was on holiday on the island.

"Every year me and my husband spend some time in Tenerife," she explained as she drove her jeep up the mountain slope. "We rent a villa, not too far from here."

"Wh-wh-wh-where's your husband now?" Linvall stammered. "Don't worry, *mon cheri*," Emmanuelle said, as she turned into a narrow country lane. "I'm sure that he is very happy enjoying himself. He will not return for some days."

Linvall sat back in the jeep with a smile on his face.

She looked so glamorous he had to compliment her.

"I like your hairstyle," he said of the neatly coiffed style assembled in a beehive do.

"Sank you," she replied, then confessed, "but it is not my hair..."

As they continued up the mountain road, Linvall got his first view of Tenerife outside Playa de Las Americas and, to his surprise it was quite pleasant and rural, but not as pleasant as Emmanuelle's hand stroking his crotch, whether by accident or otherwise, as she shifted gear.

Linvall felt his blood rush to his head and, despite himself, felt his cock stand to attention. That was the first time in ages that a woman had stroked him there, and it felt great.

"Tell me somesink," Emmanuelle said, "do you have any venereal disease?"

Linvall almost choked. He wasn't expecting that.

"N-n-n-n-no..." he spluttered.

"Good, I sink we're going to have a very interesting time," Emmanuelle smiled, patting his crotch gently. This time, it was definitely not by accident.

She turned off the road and drove up a driveway to a magnificent villa tucked away discreetly behind a cluster of conifers. Linvall whistled loudly in appreciation.

"You live here?"

"Yes, it's nice, no?"

Nice, yes, more like. Still, it must have cost a pretty penny, Linvall was thinking. He wouldn't have minded living there himself. It burned him that black folk never had this kind of cash and that the only way that a black person could get to enjoy such luxuries was to marry a white person. Well, there was one other way in which he had known brothas to sample the lifestyles of the rich and famous, and that was as a gigolo. Back in Brixton he knew a couple of rent-a-dreads, who made a nice living by turning up to rich women's houses when their husbands were out and bonking their brains out before leaving them with a very cold goodbye, an evil eye and a wad of cash in their pockets.

The maid opened the main door to let them in. Inside, the villa was sumptuous. It looked like something out of the set of *Dallas* or *Dynasty*. Linvall nodded his head approvingly and marvelled at the spiral staircase, the magnificent chandeliers that hung from the very high ceiling and the expensive furniture that decorated the place. Emmanuelle had seen it all before though, and simply took Linvall by the hand and led him up the spiral staircase to the master bedroom.

"*Mon cheri*, don't move or speak or open your eyes," she said, once they were inside.

He did as he was told. She unbuttoned his shirt to reveal a hairless chest bursting with muscles and she lowered her head and nibbled at his nipples.

"There's no need to rush," he told her as she grabbed him tightly by the bum and pulled him down onto the four poster bed.

"Oh, but there is, there is," she gushed. "I want you, and I want you now!"

"Don't worry about a thing," Linvall promised. "Steam fish and okra and mango juice built this beautiful body. Tonight I'm going to make sure you reach all the way to pleasure beach. I'm going to show you what it's like to get the wood from a black man."

"I'm married to a black man," Emmanuelle said.

"Yeah?" said Linvall surprised. "But not one like this."

"*Oui?*" she replied. "In zat case don't make any more speeches, hurry up and get on wiz it."

A generation of women have grown up dictating the terms of their sexual encounters. Emmanuelle was such a woman. Surprisingly, for a woman with all the wealth that she had, she seemed to have learned the type of English which some people might consider rude, lewd and rather vulgar. She yanked Linvall's balls and told him in no uncertain terms that it had better be as big as he said it was, because if there was one thing she couldn't stand it was a boastful man.

He smiled then sucked and pulled at her breasts. She purred as they fondled and kissed.

"My pussy's crying out for attention *aussi*," she gasped.

She reached for Linvall's zip, he pulled back.

"I just need to go to the toilet first..."

"What the f-"

"To freshen up," he said.

With a look of frustration on her face, she pointed him in the direction of the en suite bathroom.

"Can I borrow your old man's dressing gown?" Linvall asked.

"There is one in that garderobe," she said, rolling over onto her stomach to pull a cigarette out of the packet on the bedside table and lighting it.

Linvall's eyes widened when he opened the wardrobe to see a row of expensive men's suits. There must have been twenty in all. All hung very neatly and, from the labels on the lining, were all Armani.

He pulled out a silk dressing gown and took it with him to the bathroom.

The bathroom was as fabulous as the rest of the house. Gold taps and a jacuzzi were amongst its special features. For a moment Linvall stood there stark naked, admiring himself in the gilt-edged mirror above the wash basin. He smiled to himself, impressed with what he saw.

Yes, he thought to himself. He was going to control this rich woman's pussy with the most fantastic performance in bed. The first time would be strictly for him alone, frankly he didn't care whether she enjoyed it or not. He had waited too long for this opportunity for him to give her first refusal. If she was good, the second time would be for her. He would have her crying out for more to ensure that this became a very lucrative lay indeed.

He came out of the bathroom looking very smart in the dressing gown. "I wouldn't mind a suit like one of those suits your old man's got, you know."

"Yeah?" Emmanuelle replied disinterestedly, her gaze fixed firmly on what was underneath the dressing gown.

"And I wouldn't mind a nice watch either — Cartier or Rolex, I don't really mind. As long as it's heavy, you get me?"

Yes, Emmanuelle was thinking. She got him all right. But she didn't play that game.

She laughed in his face. "I don't give men money. I take it from them. Anyway, you won't need a suit to, how you say, bonk my brains out. You will be just fine with no clothes at all."

Without warning, she whipped the cord from around Linvall's waist and the dressing gown fell to the ground.

Linvall stood over her, naked as the day he was born, a big stiffie standing to attention up front, and a cheezy look on his face. His heart was pumping, his blood was rushing and he was good and ready.

Emmanuelle gave him that look that women have, the look that says, is that all there is. Linvall didn't know where to turn. That look made his dick shrink even more.

Emmanuelle lifted up his testicles carefully, as if expecting to see a Cadillac hidden underneath.

"*Merde!* Where is it?" she laughed. "A scooter can not park in my space."

It took Linvall a while to reassure her that it wasn't the size, but it was what you did with it that mattered.

"It's my prowess as a lover that you should be checking out."

Emmanuelle wasn't totally convinced but, at this late hour, she wasn't going to go without her oats.

A good session it was, too. Linvall had not enjoyed himself so much in ages. They did it in every possible position and direction. He literally found himself hanging from the chandeliers in one particularly daring move. She was giving him the right slam and, as far as he was concerned, it could go on all night long, as long as he got a chance to rest his weary manhood for an hour or so. Whether it was age or some other inexplicable reason, he was only able to manage once before he found himself needing to pause for a breather. The way he performed, it was a wonder he had had the energy to complete one time. He was trying to explain to a totally frustrated, impatient and hungry Emmanuelle, that he had to take a rest as she had chewed up his willy. "And anyway," he continued, "it's not the number of times that you make love that counts, but the quality of each session... You can't deny that it's been quality stuff."

"Well, as a matter of fact..." Emmanuelle began with obvious disappointment. She was going to tell him that she wished that sex with him had remained a fantasy and that the little there was of his willy was hardly worth chewing, but then thought better of it. She would have told him exactly what she thought of it, because she didn't have any shame, but she didn't have time for a discussion either. She simply told him in no uncertain terms that his services were no longer required and that he should get dressed and go.

"Hey!" he protested.

"Thank you very much, but I don't sink we will be doing zis again," Emmanuelle was saying, pushing him out as best she could.

"What are you, a man? You can't just bonk me and leave me," Linvall protested.

"I can and I am."

Linvall couldn't believe that she only wanted the one grind out of him. It came as a shock to discover that he wasn't the best lover that she had ever had. After all the work he put into it and all. He tried to figure out what he had done wrong, but drew a blank.

But he wasn't about to pick himself up and just leave. Without hesitation, Emmanuelle went to the phone beside her bedside and dialled a number. She spoke a few choice words of Spanish, the only word of which Linvall could pick up was "Police". She said that about three times.

"Hey, you didn't just call the cops did you?" Linvall asked.

"*Oui.* How else am I going to get you out of my house?"

Linvall still didn't believe it ten minutes later when the sound of police sirens came wailing into the drive outside. It was only then that he decided that he had better pull on his underpants, but he couldn't find them.

Now Spanish police aren't like British police. For one thing, they carry guns. And, for another thing, they don't speak English. Most importantly, they don't like the English. The policeman, with his gun drawn, was in no mood for 'reasoning' and gave Linvall exactly ten seconds to vacate the premises. Linvall could see that the ugly brute of a cop meant business. Ten seconds was too little time to search for his underpants which were lost forever somewhere amongst the bed linen. There was just enough time to grab what he could find of his clothes, but not enough time to put them on. He only just got outside the front door as the policeman, hot on his heels, reached the count of ten.

Phew!

It was only then that Linvall realized that he had his t-shirt, his socks and his shoes, but his beach shorts were still back in the house.

Blocking the doorway, the policeman glared at Linvall and shouted some abuse in Spanish, which Emmanuelle translated.

"He says, get lost and zat you better not come back here, if you don't want to spend the night in jail. He says zat he doesn't want to see you in the area again and zat, how you say, 'if you don't hear, you will have to feel'."

"What about my shorts?" Linvall protested.

"Zat's your problem, piss off," Emmanuelle translated.

"How am I going to get back to my chalet?" Linvall protested. "This is the middle of nowhere, there aren't any taxis or buses. What am I going to do?"

Again Emmanuelle translated.

"Just fuck off, how you say, 'out of it'."

It was a miserable Linvall that made his way down the path. The t-shirt tied around his waist did its best to conceal his manhood. He took one last look back towards the villa, only to see Emmanuelle caressing the policeman's balls.

It was sunset back at Las Vinas. Beres was trying to explain the difference between Chopin and Sibelius. Johnny was too busy to care which classical composer's music was oozing out of Beres' room. He had other things on his mind. He needed to get ready. He ran a cool shower to freshen up, and then spent the next hour ironing some serious creases into his trousers.

The moment of truth had come. The outfit orchestrated to perfection, a layer of dreadlocks were glued to the bald patch at the back of Johnny's head, he smelled good and his shoes were polished to a shine. He inspected himself in the mirror, and smiled a satisfied smile. His batty looked criss in these slacks. Not too African and not too Jamaican. Just criss. This was definitely going to be his night, he decided.

"As far as the Bible is concerned, men and women were made to enjoy perfect union with each other. In the Genesis account of creation, Adam was extremely pleased when God presented Eve to him and upon seeing her he exclaimed, 'This is now bone of my bone and flesh of my flesh, she shall be called woman for she was taken out of man'. Adam realised that standing before him was a woman who, though different from him, was part of him and loved her all the more for it. Hence the institution of marriage was created. As the writer of Genesis states: 'For this reason a man will leave his father and mother and be united to his wife and they will be one flesh'."

The last thing that Johnny expected to hear when he went out with a woman was quotes from the Bible. It was his domain to use the Bible to support his lifestyle, but now the good book was being used to smite him. He well wanted a jook from Jacqueline, and had even drawn his rubber out in anticipation. He had seen her sitting alone reading a book at one of the beachside restaurants and had chirpsed her straight away. She was a twenty-nine-year-old computer programmer from Luton. She was on holiday in Tenerife, but had found it boring and was looking forward to going home.

At the time he had no idea that Jacqueline devoted every Sunday to the Lord, not to mention every Monday, Tuesday, Wednesday, Thursday and Friday too (on Saturdays she went shopping, just to irritate Seventh Day Adventists). Johnny had found her charming and had hoped that it was going to be the beginning of a beautiful relationship. At least for the night. That was wishful thinking where the pentecostal cause was concerned.

"First things first," she had said when he tried to sweeten her with all his charm. "What exactly is your intention?"

"That's simple, we wine, we dine, and we grope... I mean dance. After the dance we go home to my place or yours for dessert. No problem."

"Yes problem," she replied brusquely. "You see, Eve's decision to give in to the snake's temptation and eat the forbidden fruit changed the whole nature of male and female relationships. Sin entered the equation and, ever since, has had a detrimental affect on the way men and women treat each other. Mutual equality, love and respect between the sexes have given way to male domination and female subservience. This is not what God originally intended. Furthermore, God has no intention of permitting you to get off with me tonight."

Johnny Dollar should have cut his losses and given up there and then. He knew full well that no man alive could take on H.I.M Emperor Haile Selassie I, Negusa Nagast, Lord of Lords, Conquering Lion of the Tribe of Judah, ever-living, ever-faithful — Jah Rastafari in his kingly character, and hope to survive. As futile as it seems, however, when it comes to the possibility of a little nooky, men lose their minds and start believing that they are invincible...

Jacqueline admitted to Johnny during their barefoot moonlit walk along the beach, that she had never had a serious boyfriend and that, although she had lots of male friends, she was searching for someone special in her life. Johnny suggested that meanwhile, while she was searching, they could engage in a little slap and tickle. That's when Jacqueline remembered where she had seen him before — the *Janet Sinclair Show*.

"You should have a government health warning stamped across your forehead: 'This man can seriously damage women's health'," she told him. "You need to read your Bible more often. A chapter a day. A CHAPTER A DAY! I once dated a man like you for three weeks. We could have had a serious relationship, but things went sour because I wouldn't have sex with him. Can't you irresponsible men see how you're destroying the black community? Look at the divorce rate, the rise in single parenthood and the hearts left broken by failed love affairs. Think of all the fatherless children. All this sadness, heartache and pain is a world away from the happiness and contentment God desires men and women to experience in their partnerships with one another. The Bible makes it perfectly clear, through its many pages, that God desires men and women to come together, fall in love, be faithful to one another, marry and raise children — in that order."

"Bible or no Bible, men will always be driven by hot and sweaty, rumpy-pumpy sex," Johnny argued.

"That's because you've ignored the Father's guidelines for successful human relationships and constructed your own."

"So, I suppose a blow job is out of the question?" Johnny tried hopefully.

Jacqueline maintained her cool, refusing to take the bait.

"Sex is a precious gift," she continued, "but one which God states is for marriage. It exemplifies the social, emotional and spiritual union of a couple, which is why the act is cheapened by casual sex and unfaithfulness. Sex unites couples in a deep, inextricable, irrevocable union. It is an act which says, I care for you, I am committed to you, I love you. It affects every part of an individual. I will never give away something that should only be shared with the person I am committed to by marriage."

Johnny sighed. He definitely wasn't going to get any poom-poom tonight, that was for sure. Two nights in a row without poom-poom, he thought, but still this holiday nuh finish, it nuh finish, it nuh finish...

Patrick Augustus

FLAVA IN YA EAR

Beres lay in bed awake, beside him Corinne was
sprawled naked. He had to admit, she had a beautiful
body.

Corinne still hadn't figured him out. Here she was
lying nude in bed with this fine figure of a man, yet
Beres was too busy being 'just good friends' to take
advantage of the situation. And even though she had
used all her feminine charms on him for two nights in a
row, he had still not succumbed. Nothing she did had
the desired effect of getting him to sleep with her.
Maybe he's gay, she concluded. Why otherwise would a
black man refuse point blank to take up the offer of sex
— 'no strings attached' — with an attractive woman, or
any woman for that matter?

Corinne thought she had hit the jackpot when she
invited Beres over to fix her 'plumbing'. From the
moment he stepped over the threshold there was an
immediate strange kind of electricity between them.
Her heart was pumping fast and she was good and
ready to make love for the first time in a year.
Everything seemed to be going like clockwork. She
managed to convince him to stay the night with relative
ease, and when he climbed into bed with her, she simply
lay on her back with her eyes closed and held her

breath, expecting him to take full control of the situation from there on in. Instead, he whispered into her ear, "Oh, we're not going to make love, you know."

Had she heard right? Why did he leave it to the last moment to disclose that? Was this some kind of game? Why had he not told her before she started getting moist with anticipation? How could he resist a slice of discreet no-strings-attached adult fun with a sizzling woman? He must be gay.

That first night was a frustrating night for her. She spent most of it trying to figure out a way of tearing down his resistance short of screaming, "Please, I beg you, take me... It's all yours!" She wasn't necessarily stressing him about having sex, she just wanted him to know, in no uncertain terms, that she wouldn't object to it.

Beres, on the other hand, was determined to prove that he didn't fulfil the black man stereotype. There were enough Johnny Dollars out there without him joining their club. He hadn't messed with a lot of women in his life and he wasn't about to start now. At least he had now proved to himself that he was actually capable of sleeping in the same bed with a beautiful woman and not fool around.

This was the second night in a row that they had stayed up all night just talking. The second night in a row that sex was definitely not on the agenda.

Corinne found Beres very attractive, which made it all the more frustrating. Not just attractive, but charming, sweet, considerate, intelligent, lovely personality, and a great sense of humour... Perfect! It was a long time since she had said that about any man. Why was it that a woman could save herself for a year, waiting for the right man to come along, and when he finally appeared there was an insurmountable barrier, such as his sexual orientation to overcome?

"You're different from any man I've ever met before," Corinne declared. "Nowadays it's virtually impossible to meet a black man who is more interested in my conversational skills than in sex."

In truth, Beres was as horny as the next man lying in bed with a beautiful and naked nymph. If he was reckless enough to allow his penis to do the thinking for him, he would certainly have pounced on Corinne and given her a long, hard, stiff... But what was he thinking? That was not the kind of image a buppie should be portraying. He was a new breed of black man, with good breeding. He had to make the sacrifice of not sleeping with Corinne, in order to prove to the world that there was at least one black man out there who didn't pull out his manhood to stick it in the first available hole.

This sacrifice would make him a better person, Beres was convinced of that. There was no point in trying to make his friends understand that kind of reasoning. That's why he had allowed Johnny to believe that he had made love to Corinne. The kind of man that Johnny represented just couldn't understand the meaning of such words as 'honour' and 'duty'. Johnny would never understand that Beres could still have feelings for the wife who had introduced him to her new lover on national television. All Johnny could understand was S-

Baby Father 3: *Does my batty look big in this?*

E-X.

During the two nights they had spent together, Beres and Corinne had learnt a lot about each other. She was a Gemini, born in Clarendon, Jamaica, and very frank and revealing.

"When I was married I dreamt of being single again. I yearned for the freedom and the control over my own life. Now that I'm single the one thing I miss is intimacy. Being single you get to appreciate just lying in a bed with someone. Moments like this with me and you talking. I find it hard to believe that anyone really wants to be single. If you're single there will be times when you feel great about the independence, and other times when the loneliness will hit you like a ton of bricks. I enjoy being in a good relationship. I don't want any man just for the sake of it, but I'd love to be with somebody. It's just that I haven't met anyone who qualifies...

"We were both in our early twenties and just too young to get married. There seemed to be a great urgency to get married, to live in London and start a family because we were trying to be the same as everyone else, which really is no foundation for a good relationship. We got on well to start with and were definitely in love, but we both changed over the years and, in the end, everything went wrong. Nothing could have saved it since we both hadn't finished growing up. At the time he was a sales rep for some of the top companies. He was very high powered and hated having to make time for me. It didn't help that most of the time he was pissed out of his brain. It got to the stage where he would lock himself away and not talk to me, or else we'd have endless arguments. Towards the end of the marriage he was treating me as if I was someone the cat had brought home."

All that was behind her, Corinne insisted. She had made an almighty mistake in marriage but was moving on.

He had told her about his marriages, too. About how he had tried to be the perfect husband and father. He had told her about how he used to go out of his way to do the shopping, hoovering, ironing, child-minding and washing. "On weekends there was always a cooked meal waiting at home for my wife, and I still found time to take her out afterwards. A wife is the link that makes a happy family. Each time I got married, I thought I was marrying a woman who I could love and respect and who could be my best friend."

"So how's married life treating you now?" Corinne asked.

"Not so good," Beres admitted. "We're getting a divorce..."

Corinne pointed out that they seemed to have similar stories, but Beres refused to accept that his marriages had been almighty mistakes and that he should move on for the sake of his sanity, as Corinne advised.

They were up the whole night talking, about everything under the sun. Even the most mundane things told Beres a lot about Corinne. She seemed a tad obsessive about her weight.

"I'm not fat," she said, "but I'm definitely not as thin as I'd like to be."

Beres took one glance at her naked body and thought she was just fine. He told her so, but she wasn't convinced.

"It's not only the weight that bothers me," she continued, "I hate everything about my body — my size, my shape, my height, my posture... you name it. People tell me I look great and some even say I have lovely legs, but none of that helps. I get depressed when I go into the shops and try on clothes because I never look the way I want to look in them and I never like what I see in the mirror. I'm a size 12 up top, but a size 16 down below on account of my bottom. It's embarrassing. When I come along I know that people are thinking of that old saying, 'big batty — too much pattie'."

That wasn't the way that Beres remembered the saying. The way Johnny had told it to him was more like 'big batty, tight yat...' No, not in front of a lady. Beres was too much of a gentleman for such crude behaviour. He reassured Corinne that her behind was just fine and, "Exactly the way God had intended."

They discussed many other intimate themes.

"My husband felt frustrated because he couldn't satisfy me," Corinne confessed. "Since our marriage failed, I've had a few sexual partners, but I haven't found one who can satisfy me yet," she said looking long and hard into Beres' eyes. "I guess I just find it difficult to have an orgasm. I've tried everything... the only thing I haven't tried is a man going down on me. You know how it is when you've got Jamaican partners, they never want to do that for you. I've listened intrigued when my friends have talked about it at work but I'm still waiting to find a man who's prepared to do that for me. If I could just experience that once, I'm sure I'll be able to go to my grave happy. You're not from Jamaica are you, B?"

She looked at Beres with that piercing look of hers. Beres shifted uneasily in the bed.

"No. Barbados," he admitted rather reluctantly.

The smile widened on Corinne's face.

"That's good to know," she said, "I've heard that Bajan men are particularly good 'downtown'. Is that true?"

Beres didn't want to be drawn on the issue. He chose to shower compliments on Corinne instead.

"So, why can't you find the man of your dreams? A beautiful and intelligent woman like yourself ought to have a line of men queueing for the opportunity to make you happy."

"Maybe men can spot that look of desperation on my face a mile off," she joked. "Maybe I'm just not enough of a challenge. I don't know. Why don't you answer that question on behalf of your gender group?"

Beres thought about it for a moment. He couldn't quite fathom it either.

"If you believe that there is a good man out there, he will come to you,"he assured her. "Maybe women aren't the only ones who sometimes get scared."

"I already know that, sweetheart," she said. "Hey, why get myself down, when I should be trying to get you up," she teased as her hand dived under the bedclothes and tugged at Beres' huge manhood.

Beres felt himself stiffen.

"I think it's best we just stay friends," he said hoarsely and breathlessly.

Corinne kissed her teeth. "Why do we need to be friends if there's nothing going on between us?" she asked. "I need someone to cuddle me. Give me the morning ride, B, that's what friends are for."

It had taken Linvall all night to get home semi-naked from his ordeal up in the hills. It wasn't easy trying to make it back to Playa de Las Americas with nothing to wear except a t-shirt, a pair of socks and a pair of shoes. Hitch-hiking was out of the question, he had had to keep a low profile all the way. Under cover of night, he kept close to the edge of the road and was forced to jump in a bush any time a car approached with its headlights on. By the time he arrived back in Playa de Las Americas it was already daybreak but there were still a lot of people on the streets. Covering his nakedness as best as he could, he had to inch his way forward, dodging from behind one parked car to another before he finally made it back to Las Vinas.

To Linvall's surprise, Gussie had only just arrived home moments earlier but was already sitting in the living room adding more calories to his already ample bulk with a plate piled high with chicken wings.

Gussie looked up at the sound of the front door creaking open.

"What the f-?!"

He was just about to retire for the night after an

eventful evening, the last thing he expected to see was Linvall sneaking in like a thief in the night, and trouserless to boot.

"Just don't ask," said Linvall, with his hand over his crotch. "Just don't ask, okay? I'm not in the mood."

With that he rushed upstairs to his bedroom and clothes. Gussie was sitting in the living room with a three litre tub of ice cream in front of him when Linvall came down half an hour later. Gussie scooped another heaped tablespoonful of vanilla ice cream and waited for an explanation.

"Linvall, you and I are spars but, believe me, you make me ashamed. I turn my back on you and you go off streaking in the streets. What brought this on? You can't just come home naked and expect me not to ask."

Linvall came out with the first lame excuse that he could think of.

"I got mugged," he lied.

"What, you got mugged of your clothes? They must be desperate out here. Most definitely."

"Yeah, that's right. They had knives and everything..."

Linvall sat down and concocted a perfectly viable story of how five guys in masks jumped out of the bushes as he was making his way home and robbed him, and because he was wearing all brand name designer stuff, they decided to take it all. Including his Calvin Klein briefs.

Gussie had to laugh. "I thought you were out checking some gal?"

"I was... this happened just as I left her yard."

"Well, was the sex worth it? That's the most important thing."

"Yeah, totally. As far as I was concerned, I didn't feel a way about losing my clothes because I got a good grind earlier."

"That's the way I feel, too," Gussie admitted. "I got some crazy loving tonight and I feel as if I'm a new man. You see what good sex can do for you?"

Linvall agreed. Happy to change the subject, he started talking in detail about his night's sexual adventures.

"This woman was hot, man. She was just good and ready for it. So of course I didn't disappoint."

They talked for some time in graphic detail about their sexual exploits, as men are inclined to do amongst themselves when their women aren't around. Having licked the ice cream tub clean, Gussie went to the kitchen and pulled out five packets of chocolate biscuits from the larder.

"That's the thing about married women, they just love it from any man other than their husband," Linvall said.

"So it was a married woman you were checking? I thought you were done with all that now, after the last time when the husband came home early and caught you red-handed and then proceeded to beat the shit out of you."

"You know how it is, when a woman's laying it all out for you, I just can't say no. Anyway, as far as I'm concerned, it would have still been worth it if her husband came home early. A good grind is a good grind, however painful it turns out to be."

Gussie wasn't ready to admit that he had spent the night with a married woman also. It would seem a bit hypocritical after the many times he had lectured Linvall against trespassing on another man's property. That was always a risky situation. The rules amongst men was that you stayed well away from a next man's garden and left his zone alone. You were likely to get a good smack in the face for transgressing that golden rule.

It must have been something in the Tenerife air, because back in Britain Gussie would never have behaved this badly. Maybe it was the weather which had made this woman totally irresistible. Emmanuelle was insatiable, too. She lived in a big house up in the hills and no sooner was he inside the door of her villa and the house girl had taken his coat, than Emmanuelle was upon him and literally dragged him up to the bedroom. It was like she hadn't had any sex in years. She was hot like the sun and absolutely ravished him.

It took a while for it to dawn on them both. Linvall mentioned the name Emmanuelle and Gussie's eyes lit up.

"Wait a minute, what did she look like exactly, this Emmanuelle?"

Linvall did his best to describe the chocolate coloured beauty he had engaged in penetrative sex with. Gussie couldn't believe it, didn't want to believe it…

"So, where exactly did she live?"

Linvall described her villa to the best of his ability.

"And you say you were there earlier yesterday evening."

Linvall nodded.

"So that was you, was it?" Gussie laughed.

Linvall didn't get it.

"That was you. Ha-ha. You're such a liar. Emmanuelle told me all about you... Shame! She told me that the last black man she had been with could only last five minutes, and that he was worthless and had a small needle, and that you didn't even know how to use the little you had."

"Hey! Hey...! You better watch who you're talking to like that." Linvall was fuming. Friend or no friend, he wasn't going to take that from anybody. He still didn't understand how Gussie came to all this information. "You must be talking about someone else. This Emmanuelle couldn't get enough of me. She told *me* that a splendid lover like me was just what she needed, a man who could do it all night long, who was built for comfort not for speed. She begged me to stay the night, but I refused."

Gussie couldn't stop laughing.

"So it was you, Linvall. *Shame!* Could only last for five minutes... Ha-ha..."

When Gussie finally explained the connection, Linvall was not amused.

"I hear that Guinness puts it back in you," Gussie giggled. "Drink some of that and then you wouldn't flop and your women wouldn't chat and you wouldn't have to hear this from me."

Gussie took great pleasure in boasting about how

much Emmanuelle preferred him to Linvall. She adored everything about him. She said he was the best lover she had ever had. She loved his cool profile and said that he set her heart on fire.

Linvall pointed to the beer gut that Gussie had recently developed with all his drinking and wondered what any woman would see in that.

"RAAAAS, you're a human hippopotamus!"

The two friends were becoming really irritated with each other. Such was the power of a woman to turn two amigos against one another. Linvall couldn't take any more and, even though he was dog tired, he needed to go as far away from Gussie's jibes as possible, so he went for an early morning stroll.

Linvall had been walking along the beach by himself for a couple of hours and was getting tired. He still couldn't believe why women were inclined to lie so much. He didn't care what Emmanuelle said, as far as he was concerned he had performed superbly in bed. Emmanuelle knew fully well what good sex was, and she had had plenty from him. So why did she have to lie about it? A man would never tell such an enormous fib. Men's lies in comparison were just little untruths such as: 'That was a nice meal you cooked', or 'No, you're not fat, you look criss. I can't see any cellulite, and I'm delirious with joy that your hair cost £800 and that you charged it to my credit card because it looks great, so great that I'd rather be shagging you than Naomi Campbell...' At the end of the day, women don't believe men when they tell little white lies such as: 'No, I wasn't grinding another woman last night, I was at my cousin's house discussing Marx and nuclear fission'. Whereas women are natural liars. Some men actually believe their girlfriends when they say 'Oh, it's so big'! Women used to say that to Linvall too...

This whole trip to Tenerife was coming like a soap opera. For all he knew, Emmanuelle had chatted his business to the whole town. The whole of Tenerife were probably having a good laugh at his expense at this very moment.

"Blimey, you're keen for a drink, aren't you?"

Linvall woke up and stared up into the blazing sun above. Tiredness had finally caught up with him, for he had been in a deep slumber. He had been dreaming of a thousand ways to get his revenge on Gussie for taking the piss concerning Emmanuelle. In his dream, he had first inflicted the most diseases on his friend — arthritis, diabetes, poliomyelitis, elephantitis. Then he had duped Gussie out on a rowing boat, knowing that his friend could not swim. When they were far enough out to sea, he had stood with all his weight on one side of the boat until it tipped over. In his panic, Gussie had swallowed several mouthfuls and had begged for forgiveness. "For God's sake save me, Linvall... Okay, I'm the one with the midget willy. I lied, Emmanuelle said that you were the world's best lover. It was me who she said was useless. Trust me, Linvall, you've got a gigantic dick... Please save me... don't let me drown." Linvall let Gussie go under once more before deciding to put his primary school life saving training into practice.

"Blimey, you must be desperate for a drink. How long have you been out here waiting for opening time?"

Linvall squinted his eyes. Terry the skinhead stood above him with a big grin on his face. Linvall realized that he must have fallen asleep on one of the benches outside the Traveller's Retreat. He didn't know how he had got there, but he had. He looked at his watch. It was almost noon. He must have been lying on the bench for at least a couple of hours. He could feel it in his neck and back, which were stiff and awkward.

Terry didn't waste any time in unlocking the shutters in front of the bar and letting Linvall in for the first pint of the day. As Linvall sipped on the brew, Terry busied himself by getting everything ready for opening time while he listened to Linvall drowning his sorrows in drink and telling of how this was the worst holiday he had ever been on.

"I mean, I thought Beres was a true mate, you know. You just don't know who your real friends are," Linvall was saying as Terry mopped the floor of the previous night's excesses.

It was like Linvall's tongue couldn't tell the story fast enough. Instead of returning to Las Vinas and reasoning with his bredrin about how he was feeling, he preferred to get snide and chat their business to all and sundry.

Linvall felt much more comfortable around white people than, say, Johnny Dollar. That's how it had always been. He was a product of a suburban education where he had been the only black pupil and had long got into the habit of going out of his way to show white people that he was more like them than he was a negro.

Baby Father 3: *Does my batty look big in this?*

Whenever he was chatting to a white person he would assume a cockney accent and would be the first person to say, "Look what these negroes are up to now..." In truth, Linvall was really an Englishman first and black only on the outside. Americans would call him an 'oreo', in Britain they simply say 'coconut'. And the way he was feeling now, he preferred the company of anybody else on Tenerife to that of his bonafide bredrin.

Linvall had only been moaning about his lot for about a quarter of an hour, when a heavily pregnant black woman stepped into the Traveller's Retreat.

"Blimey, baby," Terry rushed over and embraced her. "Take it easy, honey. Sit down, rest your feet. You need something to drink. Let me get you a juice, remember you're drinking for two now," Terry fussed over her. "Oh, by the way, this is Linvall, he's over here for a week. Linvall, this is my wife, Sylvia."

No wonder Terry loved his roots and culture, Linvall was thinking. He was married to a sista, and a criss one at that!

Terry returned from the bar with a glass of orange juice, which he placed on the table in front of his wife. He sat down on a stool next to her and put a loving arm around her. The couple exchanged a tender look and then, to Sylvia's obvious embarrassment, Terry started singing out of key:

> *"Black woman and child*
> *I have so much love for you*
> *Black woman and child*
> *Everything else would fade away*

> *I want to make you proud*
> *Black woman and child*
> *I swear my covenant to you always..."*

"Honestly, Terry, you're the worst singer in the world," Sylvia teased.

Terry beamed a smile as if that was the nicest thing she had ever said to him.

"You see how much she loves me," Terry winked at Linvall.

Sylvia drank a pint of orange juice before taking her leave. It was time for a siesta back home, she decided.

"That's a nice woman you've got there, mate," Linvall said as he watched her leave.

Terry nodded. The very best. "Isn't it strange how you can meet the love of your life through a lonely hearts ad."

Terry explained that he had put an advert in the lonely hearts pages of *The Voice* newspaper saying: 'Single White Male wltm Single Black Female for the world's greatest love story — EVER!' Sylvia was the first woman he dated out of the eighty replies he got and straight away he knew that she was the right woman for him, even though he did not fit into her idea of a white man. As she was a snobby Nigerian, Sylvia was expecting to date a stiff-upper lipped, theatre going, opera loving and horse riding man. Instead she found herself together with a ganja smoking skinhead who knew more about reggae and Malcolm X than she did but who, nevertheless, was willing to marry her quickly before her leave to stay in the United Kingdom came to an end. Despite the obvious problems associated with opposites attracting, the couple soon discovered that they actually loved each other and wanted to set up home together. Now, Sylvia was expecting their first child and Terry couldn't have been happier.

"You know something, Linvall," Terry was saying, as they each downed their second pint of the day, "I can't understand why so many brothas are letting the sistas down and abandoning their kids. We're supposed to be building a better world for all the youths out there. It hurts me to see all these beautiful black kids with so much talent, and all they're asking for is the same as everybody else: to have a home and family, a mother and father to call their own. Black men who aren't prepared to be a father to their children are letting the community down, man."

Linvall nodded. It hurt him to hear such words at the best time, and coming from a white man, it had a resonance that it lacked when black folk discussed the situation amongst themselves. But Linvall had been part of that very same problem, so he couldn't say anything. He thought about his own son, Lacquan, and how, for years, he had pretend that he was the boy's uncle. When he thought about it now, he couldn't understand why he had let Marcia talk him into that. It was no use regretting the past. The future was more important, and when he returned to London he would try and make it up to Lacquan by giving him all the support he needed. Why, he even had it on reliable information that Lacquan could have a promising career as a reggae deejay.

The day was getting hotter and hotter. Two things that always made Gussie hungry were good sex and heat. He had been eating almost non-stop since the previous night's sex session and he was looking forward to his second big breakfast of this sunny day. He realized he had to watch his weight though, because he could barely hold in his gut when he was out on the beach.

He had gone to the gym in the Noella Hotel across the road to Las Vinas for a quick workout so that he would feel less guilty about tucking into food all day long. The first thing that Gussie noticed at the gym, was that the Spanish attendant didn't ramp, and walked around with a can of deodorant to aim at any English tourist who made the mistake of not showering before they came for a workout. Fortunately, nothing that embarrassing happened to Gussie. Nor to the middle-aged black man on the running machine beside him.

The man was dressed in an all white track suit, with sequins and rhinestone decorations sewn on and wore dark wraparound glasses even in the gym. Had his other friends been there, Gussie would have probably laughed at this 'black Elvis'. As it was, the middle aged man had been running for half an hour at a speed of fifteen kilometres per hour, while Gussie was doing nine and struggling. After jogging for twenty minutes, Gussie could take no more and hit the 'Stop' button on his running machine. At the same time, the 'black Elvis' increased his speed to sixteen kilometres an hour.

Baby Father 3: *Does my batty look big in this?*

"What's the matter with you?" the man addressed Gussie in an American accent. "Young brotha like you ought to be able to run faster than an old man like me?"

"I'm... out... of... con-dition," Gussie gasped for air.

"Damn right. Man, you need to work that body of yours. Think of all that good pussy that's waiting for you on the beach the moment you tone your body. Let that concentrate your mind, you know what I'm sayin'?"

Gussie did know what he was saying, but right now he was more concerned about coughing his guts up. 'Black Elvis' hit the 'Stop' button on his machine and waited for the treadmill to come to a stop, before jumping off to offer Gussie some help.

"That's right, take a deep breath in... slowly... keep your head down... Think of all that good pussy that you'll miss out on if you collapse and die of a heart attack..."

That seemed to do the trick, because Gussie recovered with miraculous speed.

"Thanks," Gussie said.

"J. Douglas Jackson the third, at your service." He offered Gussie his hand. "You might have heard of me, but everybody calls me Fly. The word famous Fly..."

The man smiled, as if Gussie should know him big time. Gussie thought about it but, no, he definitely hadn't heard of him.

"You mean you've never heard of me?" Fly found it unbelievable that his name triggered no clear memory. He was sure his fame had reached over to England.

"Man, I'm so rich the President of the You-nited

States asked me for a loan. Ha-ha-ha! Can you believe that? Me — the great grandson of a slave is lending the You-nited States treasury a couple of bucks so that the You-nited States economy doesn't collapse. Ha-ha-ha!"

At first Gussie didn't believe Fly one bit. As they were getting changed together though, he started wondering. Fly dressed tackily, like someone out of a blaxploitation film from the Seventies — *Shaft*, *Superfly*, *Cleopatra Jones* take your pick — but Gussie was a jeweller, and knew enough about gold and diamonds to know that all that heavy cargo that sparkled brightly around Fly's neck, in his shirt cuffs and dripping from each of his fingers, were not only real but, indeed, high carat stuff. Fly didn't look like a 'black Elvis' any more, but looked sleek and dandy like a 'black Valentino', with a hundred grand worth of jewellery.

"Kid, you're too young to remember me when I was known as the King of the Playas," Fly said as he caught Gussie admiring his hardware. "When I started out, I was so pretty, just my ass would turn women on. All I wanted to do was bang women from coast to coast. At my peak, I was bedding 1,000 women every year. I know everything about women. In fact, I know women better than they know themselves. That's why I wear all this jewellery, because it makes women come quicker. And that's how I got the name Fly, because when I make love to women, they start singing like R. Kelly: 'I believe I can fly'.

"But being a playa's not as easy as it looks, because you can never get enough of new pussy, and where there's new pussy there's new trouble. Trauma for trauma, a playa's life is perhaps the worst type of life anybody could live. I was feared, hated and despised by my fellow men who envied what I had. A career playa like I used to be has to work literally every waking moment, sounding out potential pussy everywhere I went. It could be the young bosomy barmaid with commercial curves or it could even be your sister.

"I'm getting old now, and I don't wanna be a playa no more. I've found a woman I can lay down my life for. You see, kid, old playas never die, they either end up as raving lunatics in mental hospitals or, more generally, become preachers of the gospel."

Outside the Noella Hotel, there was a gleaming white Rolls Royce convertible awaiting Fly. At the wheel, wearing a chauffeur's peaked cap was a bikini clad '*Sun* stunner' who wouldn't have looked out of place on Page 3 of one of the English tabloid papers. In the back seat, were two other bronzed beauties.

"Yeah, I've been a playa all my life," Fly said, as he climbed into the Rolls, "but I'm definitely retiring now."

"Hey, where are you staying?" Gussie asked just as the sexy chauffeur turned the ignition of the Rolls Royce.

"Oh, I've got a little yacht moored over at the marina. It's called the 'Britannia'. I believe your Queen of England used to own it."

Gussie beamed when he heard that. Fly was the kind of man he had always dreamed about being acquainted with. He didn't want to part just yet. He wanted to get to know him and exchange business cards.

"Say, do you play dominoes by any chance?"

Patrick Augustus

The word 'dominoes' seemed to trigger a spark in Fly's mind.

"Damn right I play dominoes. Man, I've been looking all over the island for some fresh blood…"

Without further ado, Gussie invited Fly over to Las Vinas across the road. In the chalet, the sounds of The Wailers was blaring out of Johnny's room loud enough to wake up the whole of the compound. What made it worse was that Johnny was singing along to the music and, as everyone knew, he needed to take some singing lessons:

> *"Why boasteth thyself, oh evil man*
> *Playing smart and not being clever*
> *I said, you work iniquity to achieve vanity*
> *(If ah so, ah so)*
> *But the goodness of Jah Jah endureth for I-ver*
> *So, if you are the big tree, we are the small axe*
> *Ready to cut you down…"*

As Johnny lay on his bed, listening to The Wailers, he couldn't stop thinking about the group's founding member, Peter Tosh, aka Peter Touch, the Bush Doctor, the Mystic Man, the Stepping Razor' — a loved child has many names. Despite all the years that had passed since the fatal shooting of Tosh at his home in Jamaica, Johnny could still not stop the eye water from running whenever he meditated on Tosh. Johnny had met the Bush Doctor a couple of times. The last time was in Jamaica, where Tosh was keeping a distinctive low profile in the back seat of a taxi as he was then Jamaica's 'most wanted'. The police well wanted to give him some licks and kicks after certain inflammatory anti-police statements that a militant Tosh had made at the famous One Love concert back in the late seventies. To Johnny, the late great Peter Tosh was like a brother.

"Johnny, get up. I want you to meet someone," Gussie announced as he burst in. He turned down the volume of Johnny's ghettoblaster.

Johnny wasn't too keen on interrupting his meditation, but when Gussie mentioned the word 'dominoes', he was downstairs like a shot.

Despite the sunglasses that their bejeweled black American guest insisted on wearing indoors, the first thing that Johnny noticed was that Fly was a deadringer for Patrick Augustus, if a little older.

"Do you know a yout' by the name of Patrick Augustus?" Johnny asked.

"Patrick... Augustus?" Fly turned the name around in his head. "No, I don't believe I do. Is he a billionaire as well?"

Johnny had never met a billionaire before and didn't believe for one second that Fly was one, but he had met Patrick Augustus and he couldn't help thinking that the *Baby Father* author and Fly were somehow related. But Fly kept insisting otherwise, although he did say that he had heard of some guy on the island passing himself off as The World Famous Fly.

"Bwoy, you look just like Patrick you see sah," Johnny said. "Don't you think so, Gussie?"

Gussie wasn't too sure, he had been well out of it

when they had run into Patrick the other night.

"Never mind," said Johnny.

Gussie went next door and managed to persuade Corinne's room mate, Tracy, to make up the foursome. Tracy was living proof that attractive women like to hang out with unattractive women because they look even better next to them. Clearly, Tracy didn't possess any of Corinne's charm or beauty. She was flat footed and flat minded, flat chested and flat behind. She sported a pair of impressive sideburns and a couple of days' growth above her upper lip. She was also shy and quiet, but keen to show her skill at this 'man's game'. Which was just as well because none of the others even gave her sexual potential a second thought. As far as they were concerned, she was practically a man.

"Come mek we play some ketchy shuby," Johnny announced.

With that he tipped out the domino cards from their box and shuffled them around.

Fly took his dominoes very seriously indeed. For an American, he played the life or death domino style with class, slamming of cards and shouting. Johnny even paid him the compliment of playing "like a Jamaican." If anyone had the temerity to suggest that it was just a game, Fly's reply was always, "It may be just a game to you..." More than anything, Fly wanted to beat Johnny six-nil. Instead, Johnny had beaten him five-one twice and four-two three times. But none of those games gave Johnny the satisfaction that awaited him should he manage to humiliate Fly with a six-nil victory, the suggestion of which seemed to ignite the American's competitive nature.

"How about making this game a little more interesting and playing for cash?" he suggested. "Are you in or out?"

Johnny smiled. That was exactly what he was thinking. Even though Gussie tried to warn him that Fly could afford to lose a lot more money than Johnny, his friend insisted that he would show this flash geezer that it was easier for a camel to pass through the eye of a needle than for a rich man to beat a member of the Brixton Domino Association at his own game. "Go ahead, spin the wheel of your misfortune," was Johnny's famous last words to Fly.

So the gambling commenced with a double six to start and the pressure started.

CLAP! CLAP! CLAP!

"Take that. And that! And that, too."

It stopped being a game and became a war. Johnny didn't win any more games. Who would have thought that Lady Luck would turn her back on him so completely? Tracy couldn't help him either. Why should she when she was Fly's partner.

As the hours ticked by Beres came home and, seeing that his friends were engrossed in another game of dominoes, simply said a quick 'Hello' to Fly then left in a hurry. Linvall also returned from his early drinking session, reeking of booze and declaring that there was a gleaming white Rolls Royce parked outside with three criss women in it.

Gussie explained that the car belonged to Fly and that Linvall should stick around, because he might be able to learn one or two things about how to deal with women from a man who knew women better than they knew themselves. Linvall simply kissed his teeth and cut his eye at Gussie, before taking his seat at the domino table, just in case there was anything to be learned.

Five hours later, Fly had beaten Johnny six-nil six times and was three grand in profit. Johnny had not only used the money that he had earned selling the Bibles, but he had also signed away all the traveller's cheques he had brought with him for his holiday spending money. It was too late to stop gambling now. He couldn't let Fly take his hard earned money and leave, he had to win it all back.

"Ready for round two? One more game?" Johnny asked.

"Damn real," Fly replied. "I'ma keep rollin'. Hell yeah."

"Double or nothing, winner takes all," Johnny suggested. "Only, I'm a little light on cash, can I give you an I.O.U.?"

Fly couldn't believe what he was hearing.

"Lemme explain something. This is not Monopoly, kid. Cash rules. Money talks, bullshit walks. Understand this: There are winners, and there are losers. What are you gonna be? This is Tuff Street. Around here we play for keeps. Look kid, there's gonna be a time when you get a chance to win. When that time comes, you're gonna have to go out there and kick somebody's ass, like I've kicked yours. But today's not that time. You gotta spend money to make money. I'm talking dinero, mullah, cash dollars, greenbacks, the hard stuff, bread, monetary units, sweet cream... Positively no credit cards, no I.O.Us..."

It was then that Fly revealed to all assembled that he had made his vast fortune by gambling. As he scooped all the money he had won from Johnny off the table into his pockets, Fly explained that he was the man who had broken the bank at the casino in Monte Carlo to make his first million, and since then he had gambled on the stock market with the expertise of King Midas.

"People are always trying to probe the money-making skills they believe are buried inside my skull. You want me to tell you the secret of becoming a fabulously rich man like myself?"

Gussie nodded eagerly.

"Well, in the cold-blooded academy of ghetto streets, I was taught early that men have more hair than women, but on the whole women have more than men." Fly burst out laughing. "Geddit? On the 'hole' women have more hair than men..." Again he cracked up with laughter, savouring his own joke. "Okay, I was only kidding. What the ghetto streets really taught me was that understanding women is necessary for an aspiring black man trying to make it in life. Love and fabulous wealth don't mix, so it's one or the other — the choice is yours. My advice is do like I did when it comes to women, stay cold and brutal and never try to keep them happy when it's difficult enough to keep yourself happy. Women will laugh at you otherwise and take advantage of you. Life is not a beauty contest, you know. In real life, however much you think a woman loves you, let me tell you, there are playas out there in the streets who can lay your woman and suck her pussy so good she'll have convulsions with diarrhoea! You think she's going to love you after that? No, man. Don't ever play that bullshit love stuff. You've got to control the pussy. You've got to be the boss of your woman's life, even her thoughts. You've got to con them that Lincoln never freed the slaves. Keep them conned, confused, bamboozled and fascinated by humping the living daylights out of them. But never, and I mean NEVER, get emotionally attached to them. Believe me, I know, the way you start with a woman is the way you end with a woman."

Gussie nudged Linvall in the ribs. "You hear that Lickle Linvall? I hope you're taking heed of what Fly's saying. Most definitely. By the way, Linvall, did I tell you that Emmanuelle gives a good blow job too? But you wouldn't know about that would you, because you got dissed before you got a chance to really savour her pleasures. Most definitely."

"Get off my tits, man," Linvall warned, feeling very awkward.

"Yeah, that's what Emmanuelle said to you last night, wasn't it. Hear what, little Linvall, SPIT IN YOUR OWN BOWL! Emmanuelle belongs to me."

"Wait a minute..." Fly interrupted. "This Emmanuelle, does she live in a big villa up in the hills?"

"Yeah, that's the one," Gussie grinned. "Linvall only lasted five minutes in bed with her. I had to go there later to show her what good sex was about."

"You mean you were FUCKING MY WIFE!" Fly

exploded, jumping to his feet.

"W-w-w-w-wife?!" Gussie could barely get the words out of his mouth. "B-b-b-b-bu..."

At that moment, Corinne from next door tapped on the glass pane of the patio window.

Relieved at the opportunity to diffuse the situation, Beres got up quickly to let her in.

"Have you seen, Beres?" she asked. "My plumbing needs fixing again."

At the sight of this attractive woman who he had not yet bedded, Fly took on a whole new persona and seemed to forget all about Linvall and Gussie's transgression. He went up to Corinne and, with a bow of his head, held her hand delicately in his and kissed it.

"My word," he beamed, "God has made you the most perfect of all His creations. If He allows me to indulge in you, I would be the luckiest man alive. May I ask to whom I am addressing?"

Corinne was taken aback by Fly's chivalrous approach and speech, but a little twinkle in her eyes said that she approved of it.

"Corinne," she answered softly.

"Ahhhh, Corinne..." Fly repeated as if he was savouring a Cordon Bleu meal. "It's a lovely thing to meet someone as beautiful as you. Now Corinne, I know you women say that we guys always use the same lines, but I would be very interested in finding out more about you. If you allow me to do so, I am sure you will find that there's no speech and no language which I do not understand."

"Haven't I seen you somewhere before?" Corinne

asked.

"Your probably have. J. Douglas Jackson the third, at your service." Fly bowed again. "But everybody calls me Fly. The word famous Fly."

"Oh, yes I remember now, you're the man who broke the bank at Monte Carlo."

"The one and the same. So, sexy lady, let's get it on. What is your desire, what is your request? If you give me the honour, I would like to dine with you on my yacht. It's called 'Britannia'. You may have seen it, your Queen Elizabeth of England used to own it... So how about it?" he offered Corinne his arm. "Will you join me for dinner? I'm sure a bottle of the most expensive champagne would go down well with the meal."

Corinne hesitated.

"Oh come on," Fly insisted, "you know your pussy is jumping for me, so take up the offer before some other lucky bitch steals me from you."

Corinne didn't hesitate any longer. She took Fly by the arm and accompanied him out of the house.

"Bwoy, did you see dat!" Johnny exclaimed. "The man walks in our yard, him teef all my money an', before I get a chance to win it all back, him just ah rope in an' control Beres' t'ings. Dat nuh right, man. Dis t'ing yah nuh finish, it nuh finish, it nuh finish..."

BUST A RHYME

The monkey speaks his mind...
Two sat in the coconut tree
Discussing things as they seemed to be
Said one to the other, 'Now, listen you,
There's a strange rumour that can't be true
That man has descended from our noble race.
That would be a big disgrace...'
Yeah, the monkey always speaks his mind.

To fornicate, or not to fornicate that was the question that had been playing on Beres' mind all evening. Whether it was nobler in the mind to suffer the slings and arrows of outrageous fortune by resisting temptation or whether he should just get on with it and bonk the living daylights out of Corinne as she would like him to do.

He had needed to be alone to do his thinking, and had just kept walking along the beach until he found a little deserted cove where he was able to sit on the sand meditating all day and all evening, watching the tide roll in.

Ask most men what they would like for Father's Day, and they'll probably tell you a new woman: 'It's like food... when you eat chicken every day, you yearn for a good steak for variety'.

But Beres wasn't most men. He was a new breed of modern 21st century black male who, up until now, believed that sexual exclusivity was possibility in marriage or a steady relationship and that monogamy was still the best form of marriage. But now, he wasn't too sure.

When Beres thought of marriage, the poignant part of the traditional vow that came to mind were: 'forsaking all others' and 'until death do us part'. Until now he had always believed that romance coupled with sexual exclusivity was the ideal for a marriage, but he was no longer sure whether it was the reality in modern life. After all, the divorce rate was soaring, and serial monogamy, by way of divorce and remarriage, was becoming increasingly popular as was extramarital sex and the single-parent family.

By now, most men would have wanted to give Beres a good hard slap. They wouldn't have been able to relate to his discourse of whether he should or he shouldn't. For most men, there was no question of hesitation at the offer of sex on a platter.

For Beres, on the other hand, sex went deeper than just 'wham, bam, thank you ma'am'. It was a question of the right chemistry between two people, and not a question of being able to bump an' grind solidly for three hours. In Beres' experience, it was usually more satisfying fantasising about a woman than actually having sex with her.

To fornicate, or not to fornicate...

Baby Father 3: *Does my batty look big in this?*

Beres wouldn't even be sitting on a rock on a deserted beach in Tenerife considering the question if Sonia hadn't left him in the first place.

For years Christianity has espoused the principle that one spouse for life is the highest form of marriage and a mark of advanced civilization. That is exactly what Beres believed when he first got married, but he had subsequently learned, through heartbreaking trial and error, that that wasn't the case at all. At all, at all...

When he and Sonia first met, he did everything in his power to ensure that it was all hugs and kisses and sunshine and everything else. If he was astute enough to interpret the dark clouds that loomed over Sonia's head, he wouldn't have got involved.

In the beginning, everything was fine and dandy and their relationship was sheer sweetness. But something happens to women after they get married, Beres reflected, and he should know because he had been through the marriage ceremony twice now and each time there was a fundamental 'before and after' change in his spouse. He didn't know what it was, but from the moment that wedding ring was slipped on their finger, each wife started ordering him around and expecting him to have gone to work and earned money on their behalf. Beres had done all of that. He was prepared to sit down and make it work even when things got rough. Sonia got pregnant and they had a kid and it looked like they were going to live happily ever after. Yet Sonia ended up suddenly announcing, "I don't know if I want to be married any more..." As if you could treat marriage like it was a career that you could change the moment you got tired of it. Sonia may as well have said, "I don't love you any more... I don't know if I ever loved you."

Even their friends believed that Beres and Sonia were the perfect buppie couple, so it wasn't so surprising that Beres almost collapsed when his wife told him that she had been having an affair. Then she informed him that her lover was a woman!

It still hurt so bad when he thought about it. It wouldn't have been as bad if she had had an affair with another man, he could live with that, but having sex with another woman was like telling him that he didn't suffice as a man.

Even after he married Caroline, the fact that his first wife had left him for another woman still bugged Beres. Somewhere deep inside of him, he wanted just one more opportunity to prove to Sonia that he was a real man. One hundred percent Caribbean man! He couldn't get it out of his head. So when the opportunity came along he had to take it. It wasn't a question of greed, he knew Caroline was a nice woman and he didn't need to go outside for hamburger when he had steak at home, yet he had to stop blaming his male virility for driving his first wife into the arms of another woman.

Woe is the man who tries to have his cake and eat it, too. Beres thought he could get away with it but, in the event, he had ended up losing Caroline as well. If only he had considered the one night stand with Sonia thoroughly as he had been considering this possible fling with Corinne, he may have better summed up the consequences. In which case he wouldn't be sitting here feeling sorry for himself as he and Caroline would still be an 'item'.

On the other hand, what had been done had been done, there was nothing he could do about it. He didn't intend to spend the rest of his life living in hope that Caroline would come back to him. He had to keep on moving. Like anybody else, he needed a dose of TLC every now and then and, for that, he needed a woman. At his age, it was dangerous pining for a woman. In a year or two he wouldn't be able to say that he was in his mid-thirties any more, he would have to admit that he was in his late-thirties or, worse, approaching forty. For each new year, Beres knew, his marketability on the singles scene would diminish. The longer he waited for a 'happily married life' to happen, the more he increased his chances of missing the boat. What self-respecting man wanted to go into his forties, sitting in a pub on his own, pining for his ex-wife?

To fornicate or not to fornicate...

It was after midnight by the time Beres decided to let his carnal instincts get the better of the argument. At the end of the day, he concluded, the sky wasn't going to come crashing down on his head if he had sex with Corinne. He was tired of staying up all night, fantasizing about the most unpleasant things in order to control the libido which was threatening to embarrass him with a hard and stiff. Besides, it didn't take a genius to take one look at the world and conclude that, contrary to Beres' beliefs, it did not seem that men and women were by nature monogamous. It was nothing to do with right or wrong or 'to fornicate or not to fornicate'. It just was.

Give a man a reason to be unfaithful, and he'll take it. Give him numerous reasons and he'll dance a jig and sing 'tra-la-la-la-la-la-la-la-lee' and justify his actions perfectly each time. Beres spent the next hour on that secluded beach ticking off a number of excuses and whistling happily to himself.

For one thing, the experiences of fidelity, had caused him too much pain, mistrust, anger and alienation (when he thought about it, that wasn't one excuse, but four).

For another thing, those of his friends who fornicate regularly all affirm that it reduces stress levels and promotes personal growth and a sense of identity. Accepting the fact that none of us is truly monogamous, Beres reasoned, was an adult way of looking at relationships without having to torture yourself.

Then you had to consider the fact that every man has a tiger in his tank. It is in the nature of the beast to wander and it is unlikely that the beast in any man will ever be tamed.

One more thing. Despite his perfect 'New Age Buppie' credentials, Beres was basically a horny man and had now reached the conclusion that there was nothing he could do about that.

Beres got up and dusted down the sand from his Gap khakis and looked at his watch. It was way past midnight. It had taken him almost eight hours to come to the conclusion that to fornicate was no big deal. Tonight, Corinne was going to get exactly what she had been asking for. He was going to give her the most pleasure. It made him hard and stiff to even think about it.

Half an hour later, Beres slipped into Corinne's chalet by twisting the doorknob upwards in the way she had shown him, and let himself in. It was dark inside, except for the lamp in the living room which was always left on. Silently, he made his way upstairs. She was obviously asleep, because when he opened her bedroom door gently, it was completely dark inside. He stripped immediately and fumbled in the dark to find the hook behind the door to hang his khakis neatly. Then he slipped into bed beside her. This time, he was good and ready for it. He slipped his arm around her naked body and reached for her breasts. Nice and much larger than he had imagined, they felt like heaven. He had never imagined that she would feel so nice, so loveable, so desirable...

She stirred in her sleep and mumbled something.

"It's all right," he whispered in her ear softly. "It's only me, Beres. I can't make any promises, but I want to help you rediscover your trust in men. Just relax."

The sexual pull he felt towards her was as powerful as ever. His manhood started growing longer and harder and longer and harder until, without any push or effort on his part, it eased itself towards her as it grew. Suddenly, as it touched her bottom, her body

125

stiffened and she sat bolt upright in the bed.

"Beres?" she said.

She reached for the bedside lamp and switched it on.

Beres screamed. She screamed. But *she* wasn't Corinne. *She* was Lesley, Johnny Dollar's baby mother number one.

"Wh-wh-wh-what are you doing here?" Beres gasped.

"What are *you* doing here," she replied, equally mystified.

"W-w-where's Corinne?"

"Who is Corinne?"

"The woman who was living in this chalet earlier today."

"Oh, the two women who were staying here moved out, apparently to go and spend the rest of their holiday on a yacht."

"B-b-b-b-b-b-b-but-but-but..."

Beres knew he wasn't making much sense. Grabbing a pillow to cover his nudity as best as he could, he fell out of the bed and tripping over the bedclothes, rushed to his feet and grabbed his trousers from behind the door.

"I thought... I didn't know... I..."

He finally managed to get his trousers on and bolted out of the bedroom, still apologising. He fell down the stairs and tumbled outside the front door and didn't stop running until he was safely in his own chalet next door, with the front door bolted tightly behind him. He turned to see Linvall sitting in the living room, nursing a bruised eye.

126

Linvall's cock had told him to go and check Tracy, Corinne's room mate, for a grind. He couldn't take the fact that there were two women next door and he was lying in his bed alone. He had tried to get to sleep, but unsuccessfully. It was one of those hot, sultry, tropical nights when if you weren't getting a grind, you couldn't get to sleep. The thought of rubbing up against Tracy was just irresistible. Anyway, hadn't Gussie told him that he had bumped into Tracy earlier on in the day and she had said that she had watched Linvall several times from her bedroom window, and that she fancied him bad and that she wouldn't mind proving that to him in bed with her tongue! Gussie made it clear that this was a virtual green light for Linvall to go over and check her any time, even with his wee willie winkle. Linvall could have hardly been expected to pass up such an opportunity.

Beres had told him how he usually jiggled the doorknob to get in next door, and Linvall had done likewise. He had made his way quietly upstairs and tiptoed into the darkened bedroom, casting off his clothes as he entered. From past experience, he knew that it wasn't good to give a woman the opportunity to decline. He didn't want any chatting, considering or second thoughts, he wanted to get straight down to business and deal with the matter at hand. Naked, he eased himself into the bed beside her and slipped his arms around her waist. He soon found his hand wandering up towards her breasts. He kissed her neck

127

tenderly and breathed seductively into her ear. Finally she began to stir. Half asleep she mumbled something.

"What was that?" Linvall asked softly and tenderly.

"Is that you Linvall?"

Linvall smiled. "Yes, it's me, Linvall. The man of your dreams."

Suddenly, he felt an elbow dig sharply into his face.

"Aaaaagh," he cried out, falling out of bed and rolling over in pain.

The bedside lamp came on. When Linvall saw the vicious look on the face of his wife, Marcia, all he could do was scream and keep on screaming, as if he had just seen a werewolf.

But his screaming had no effect on Marcia, who proceeded to slap him down with a left and a right and a left, bobbing and weaving as she fired a thousand questions at machine gun speed, all the time floating like a butterfly and singing like the queen bumble bee.

"What are you doing in this bed? Who did you think was in the bed with you? Were you having an affair with the previous occupant of this room? Why else would you have slipped into the bedroom without knocking on the door first? Is that a hickey on your neck? So, you have a woman out here? Do you think I'm stupid?"

Linvall was still paralyzed with shock. He was extremely nervous because he could see in Marcia's eyes that her bullshit detector was scanning his face for the slightest trickle of cold perspiration. When he eventually spoke, his answers came slowly and cautiously.

No, he knew she wasn't stupid, nor did he think that she was born yesterday. He didn't know how he had got there. Isn't that strange, after all these years he hadn't even realized that he sleepwalked. Of course he wasn't having an affair. "Honestly, I don't know no one over here," he pleaded. "Anyway, why would I want an affair when I'm having all this great sex at home?"

"With whom are you having all this great sex?" Marcia snapped.

"Why, with you, dear apple of my eye, oh one and only vibrator of my loins."

It's amazing how poetry just seems to trip from men's tongues when they're under manners, or in Linvall's case, under heavy manners.

Marcia searched Linvall's face closely. She claimed that 'I've Been Playing Away From Home' was written all over his face, but conceded that she had not yet caught him red-handed, but that didn't mean that she believed him for one second. She was a true believer in the notion that all men were dogs, and that once a dog always a dog. It was just a matter of time before she caught him red-handed, she promised.

"You look like you've been dealing with a white woman," she suggested.

On that, Linvall was confident enough to cross his heart and hope to die.

Still, Marcia wouldn't be satisfied until she had carried out a dickie inspection.

"Right, drop your pants," she ordered.

Back in their chalet next door, Beres was still gasping for breath having bolted from the 'incident' with Lesley.

"You're never gonna believe this…" Beres began.

"No, you're never gonna believe what I'm going to tell you…" Linvall interrupted. He was still in a state of shock after having brought his cock home in a hurry.

Even when they had both told each other their identical news, they still had to pinch themselves to be sure that they weren't sharing the same dream. One thing they didn't dare do, was go next door for a second opinion.

Johnny's opinion was that women were often too facety for their own good, not least those he met in his dreams. Like the nightmare he had tonight, a reminder, if any were needed that while a lot of men think they've been forgiven for their misdemeanours, their wives are actually hatching complicated and luxurious plans for when the children have grown up.

Tonight's nightmare went *black* to the future, the year 2020. Johnny was middle-aged. His years of sampling a 'trailerload ah gal' was over, the groupies and other ladies with a voracious sexual appetite had long moved on in search of younger, more nubile pastures (while Viagara had once and for all solved the problem of impotency, it had neither made older men more attractive nor had it given them the health, strength and energy of a twenty-year-old which, after all, was what women wanted even in the year 2020). Yet, despite his receding hairline, Johnny approached the twilight of his active sexual life with a happy face, a thumping bass and a mild case of 'nostaminaitis'. Even though the days were gone when all he had to do was click his fingers and the ladies would come running, Johnny was still to be found at the discos of the future in the vain hope that somebody's daughter would have a penchant for older men who still had it in them — once a month.

Well, not so vain hope. Not tonight, anyway. Tonight, he was going home with the crissest little sex machine in the house. Her name was Chantelle, she was brown and slim, and he was looking forward to dropping a good grind on her later.

Johnny snorted and leaned back with a triumphant smile as Chantelle's ample bosom hypnotised him from within her itsybitsy blouse. She wore long, silky green hair, green lipstick and green contacts and oozed sexual gratification. It was reassuring to know that that old feeling was still lurking in his loins. What could be more satisfying for a man his age, than knowing that this sex kitten had chosen him amongst all the muscle men in the disco who were half his age?

When he was done contemplating the very real possibility of savouring what he had only had the opportunity to fantasize about in the past few years, the disc jockey brought the music to an abrupt end.

"Ladies and gentleman," he announced in his microphone, "as it's old school revival night, let me introduce one of the leaders of the old school... From back in the day when there were two kinds of men: real men and cocks men. He himself, is a cocks man extraordinaire with a minuscule brain in the head of his cock, but no control over said organ. Such is this cocks man's insatiable appetite that, tonight, he's hoping to get some poom-poom from his own daughter and he doesn't even know it... Ladies and gentleman, let me introduce the Original Cocks Man — Johnny Dollar!"

On cue, a spotlight bathed Johnny in a sea of glaring light. He took a closer look at Chantelle who had now pulled the wig from her head and was aiming an AK47 between Johnny's balls. A pained look came over his face, as if someone had clumsily ripped the lace off his lavender see-through shirt. He now recognized the teenage girl that he was trying to get off with, as the youngest of his eighty-four pickney by eighty-three different women. How was he to know, he hadn't seen her in years due to the ignorance of her mother...

"Trying to sleep with your own daughter is an abomination to the Lord," Chantelle admonished. Everybody in the disco (Johnny excepting) applauded, nay, cheered. Chantelle continued. "It says in the Bible, 'If your right hand offend you, cut it off'. And like my mum's always telling me, your cock is so offensive, it would save a lot of heartache all round if it was cut off."

Johnny stared at his daughter with glazed eyes. His breathing became erratic, coming in short, sharp bursts. He clutched at his heart and begged her, "I know how you feel, I wasn't always there for you as a father, but please don't..."

She simply sneered. "This is not about my feelings. This is about reality. This is about the problem that's destroying our community, and when you find the root of a problem you have to cut it off. That's the bottom line. Like my mum's always telling me, it would be doing the world a favour to separate your cock from your balls."

"Please, Chantelle," Johnny couldn't even remember her real name, due to the mother's lengthy enforced separation of father from daughter, so for the moment her assumed name would have to suffice. "For the love of Jah, please don't shoot me in the balls. I'm your own flesh and blood... You're my seed..."

"Oh no you don't, motherfucker! My mum always said that you would always try to resist castration. Trust me, the baby father ain't been pulled out of his mama's womb who can escape retribution from his baby mother and child."

With that she squeezed the trigger and Johnny awoke from his nightmare with an agonizing pain in his testicles.

It was a terrible state of affairs. When Johnny limped down to breakfast the next morning, Gussie, Beres and Linvall were sitting on the sunny patio, eating a light breakfast of ripe mangoes and fruit juice.

Johnny thought that Linvall was joking when he said, "Hey Johnny, your baby mother's next door, you know."

Instinctively, he had replied, "That's all right, all my baby mother's know their place. Skeen?"

"I heard that!" came a cry from the open window of one of the upstair's bedrooms next door.

Johnny wasn't too sure. The voice sounded vaguely

like Lesley's, but surely it wasn't possible? He wouldn't be able to eat any breakfast until he had limped next door and found out.

No sooner had he knocked on the front door of the neighbouring chalet than his suspicions were aroused. For, to his surprise, the door was opened by Marcia Henry, Linvall's wife.

"Oh... it's you," Marcia said, looking Johnny up and down disdainfully. Then she called over her shoulder, "Lesley, your wotless baby father's here!"

"Hey, hey, hey!" Johnny retorted. "Enough of that slackness. Skeen?"

He would have given Marcia even more of an earful, if Lesley hadn't appeared behind her, dressed from head to toes in an African style outfit and with her hair covered by a headwrap. She didn't seem at all surprised to see him.

"Wh-wh-wh-wh..." Johnny could only stare. There was something different about Lesley. He couldn't put his finger on it, but more importantly how could he have come all the way to Tenerife, only to find that his woman was living next door?

Yes, there was definitely something different about Lesley, Johnny concluded as he followed her up the stairs to her bedroom. It wasn't just the calm and peaceful manner in which she spoke to him or the way she held her head high and her back as straight as an arrow when she walked. It wasn't just the lack of make-up on her face, or the proliferation of underarm hair. Lesley had a certain aura about her now, which Johnny could only describe as regal.

Baby Father 3: *Does my batty look big in this?*

"Baby, it's so good to see you here in Tenerife," Johnny lied.

"Johnny, I don't have much time, you said there was something really important that we had to discuss in private. So here we are in my bedroom…"

"I just wanted to say that, believe me, I never knew that bitch was going to go live on the *Janet Sinclair Show* and tell the whole world that she was ex-ex-ex-ex-ex-ex…"

Johnny struggled with the words. But found it hard to say. He tried again.

"She told the whole world live on the *Janet Sinclair Show* that she was ex-ex-ex-ex-ex-ex…" Try as hard as he could he just could not get the word out, and the stammer was making it sound like he was saying 'sex-sex-sex-sex' rather than struggling with the first two letters of the word 'expecting' Why was he finding it so hard to confess to Lesley that a next woman was expecting a child by him? He tried several more times to say the word, but finally he couldn't take it any more and simply blurted out: "I have a next child coming… But before you say anything, there are two sides to every story. I never even knew she was pregnant… It was just a one shot t'ing, y'know how it go… I can't make those women not try to seduce me."

Lesley took in what Johnny had to say. Then she sat down on her bed — in the lotus position, and for the next few minutes just breathed in and out deeply. Then she confessed that this was the first she had heard about Johnny's appearance on the *Janet Sinclair Show*. She had got his note saying that he had gone on a fishing trip, that was the last she had heard from him before

"B-b-b-b-but I thought word had got to you on the streets?"

Lesley reminded him how totally unscientific and inefficient the ghetto grapevine was. "Still," she concluded, "it's better to hear such news from the horse's mouth."

Johnny couldn't believe that he had exposed himself unnecessarily. If Lesley hadn't heard about the *Janet Sinclair Show*, he wouldn't have had to confess and wouldn't have to deal with the fury, frustration and recriminations that would surely follow.

To Johnny's surprise, Lesley didn't seem to care about the fact that the father of her children was expecting yet another child by yet another woman. Still in the lotus position, she simply breathed in and breathed out deeply then told him in no uncertain words that he could carry on with his foolishness as long as he wanted to. It was no longer any of her business.

"What do you mean by that? Of course it's your business," Johnny retorted. "Didn't you hear what I said, yet another outside woman is expecting yet another yout' by me. That's going to affect our relationship. It's going to affect the two pickney we already have together. Can't you see that? It's going to mean that the CSA will be on my case and that will mean I've got even less cash to spend on the pickney I already have."

"You should have thought of all of that before you let your loins do your thinking for you," Lesley replied calmly. "I used to think that I was tied to you by the hip, Johnny, and that whatever you did would affect me. But now I realize otherwise. I'm a new black woman, Johnny. I am a princess of the universe. I now know that I don't need a man like you and that my children don't need a father like you. How do you think your children feel when the whole of Brixton is talking about how many kids by different women their father's got? Don't you think it affects your daughter when even the Brixton police know her father as the 'Original Baby Father'? No, Johnny, our children can live without you and I can live without you. The sista that I used to be always believed that my black man could improve. Now I realize that he can't. Spreading your seed is the best you can do. It's not much to shout home about, is it Johnny?"

Johnny didn't know what to say. He spluttered something about having undiscovered talents other than that, but he didn't even convince himself with that argument. Okay, fair cop, he conceded, he had a fourth child coming by a third woman, but that shouldn't affect the great relationship that he had with Lesley, should it?

"Well, I'm afraid it does matter," Lesley said firmly. "You see, I'm looking for a clean slate. Johnny, I'm giving you complete freedom," she continued returning to her serene and regal manner, "you're always complaining that relationships always make you feel like you've got a ball and chain tied to your testicles. Well now you can have as much freedom as you need. I won't be troubling you again…"

Lesley was right, freedom had been what Johnny had spent many waking hours fighting for. That was exactly what he needed. With freedom he could go out and chirps as many women as he wanted to and not have to cover his tracks. With freedom, he could even check women and then come home to his main woman and tell her of his sexual adventures without her getting upset. That was the kind of relationship he had always wanted, but now that it was being handed to him on a plate, it felt bitter-sweet. For one thing, why was Lesley giving him all this freedom without the customary struggle? And another thing, there was a certain finality in her tone which worried him.

No, on reflection, it was better if he didn't touch that freedom at all, he reasoned. It suddenly dawned on him that having children was a serious thing and that he had to be a responsible father. Okay, he couldn't help the fact that another one was on the way. He would have to be there for that child also, because what kind of father would he be otherwise? "I'm not saying I was right, but you must remember, Lesley, I'm a mortal man, and what happened wasn't intentional, I was caught in a certain situation. What's done is done," he said loftily. "I can't turn back the hands of time. That's just the way my life has worked out. If I had my chance again, I would make sure that I didn't have children by three different mothers. But it happened, and now I have to live with it. Me and you have to live with it, Lesley. Me, you and the kids have to live through it. And if my youts end up saying, this is all daddy has done with his life, I won't be able to deny it. All I can do is be a lot more careful in future. From now on, I will always make sure that I use a double thick condom. I might even use two double thick ones — just in case."

Brave is the knave who steps up to be slayed by the one who forgave him for his first mistakes. Fortunately for Johnny, Lesley didn't see that condemning him yet again would lead anywhere.

"When you destroy my life, don't you know you're destroying yours too? You can't keep me down without keeping yourself down," she told him. "You eroded my self-confidence with all your philandering. But now I know who you are, I've made up my mind that I'll get on without you. Johnny, take your life and go and live it outside of my postal district. Me and the children don't care if we never see you or hear from you again."

There was something in the calm manner in which Lesley was saying all of this which made Johnny realize that this time she meant exactly what she said, and he didn't like it one bit.

"Okay, I'm not infallible," he pleaded with her, "I done you wrong, but I'm only human. Who is perfect? I don't know one person who is perfect. Lesley, can't you see, I don't want to be free... I love you, I want to be with you and my children. Baby, I'm sorry, please believe me."

Even as he spoke Lesley closed her eyes in meditation and then started chanting in ancient tongues as a stream of consciousness consumed her.

When she opened her eyes, she told Johnny very calmly, "Sorry is the only thing you can say, after all the destruction you have created. Sorry won't ease the pain.

You have betrayed me for the final time. Let me spell it out for you: l-o-v-e d-o-n'-t l-i-v-e h-e-r-e a-n-y m-o-r-e."

Why did women always terminate a relationship by saying that, Johnny wondered.

"Love definitely don't live here any more," Lesley repeated contemplatively. "Love ain't ever going to live here again, neither. All that remains is emptiness... I don't want to hear anything you've got to say. I told you many times that I wouldn't put up with your behaviour indefinitely, but you don't listen to anything I tell you. Now you're coming to me with tears in your eyes, but it's too late.

"L-o-v-e d-o-n'-t l-i-v-e h-e-r-e a-n-y m-o-r-e."

There she goes again... Lord have mercy!

It could only mean one thing if she didn't want him around, Johnny deduced, Lesley must be checking some other man. Why else was she so willing to give the father of her children his freedom without putting up a spirited struggle?

"You're having an affair, aren't you?" he challenged.

Lesley frowned.

"Yeah, *right.* I met a man at a party and he was exciting. He was handsome and charming and rich, and he drives me in flashy cars to expensive hotels for exciting sex sessions..."

Johnny didn't need to hear any more. His suspicions were confirmed. He burst into tears.

"I forgive you," he sobbed. "There's no question, I forgive you , I still love you and I want you back."

"Oh, thank you very much," Lesley said with exaggerated irony. "Look Johnny, get real. Thanks to you, it's going to be a long time before I am going to feel good about going to bed with any man or even date a man. That's how much your behaviour has put me off the whole of *man*kind. From now on, I will take my strength from my universal sisterhood. You take one twig and you try to break it, it snaps easily, but if you take a whole bunch of twigs and you put them together, they are much harder to break. That's how it is with us sistas of the universe."

Johnny thought about Lesley's words for a moment. "You're starting to sound like a lesbian," he said. "What happened to you?"

Lesley picked a book up off the bedside table so quickly, that Johnny didn't even see her fling it. But it struck its target between his eyes with a thud.

After rubbing the bridge of his nose better, Johnny picked up the purple book and read its front cover: *Acts of Faith*, by Iyanla Vanzant...

Apart from his close shave with Lesley, Beres wasn't too troubled by the arrival of Johnny and Linvall's baby mothers in the middle of their holiday. Sure, it would cramp their style, but it wasn't his lookout. After all, it wasn't his woman who had moved in next door. For him, it would be business as usual. He would continue enjoying himself for the remainder of the week.

He had gone into the Hotel Tenegrief to change some of his money as he had done every afternoon since arriving. Beres was one of those cautious holidaymakers who only changed his traveller's cheques bit by bit every day, just in case the value of the pound went up against the local currency and he was able to profit by a few pennies.

For some inexplicable reason, Beres was humming the nursery rhyme about "four and twenty blackbirds baked in a pie" as the hotel receptionist counted out his pesetas. He picked up the money and tucked it into the pocket of his multicolour Hawaii shirt. Just as he was about to leave, he heard a familiar voice behind him. His heart started pumping as he turned slowly around to see Caroline, his wife, ordering a hotel porter around in typical confrontational barrister style, as to where to put her luggage and how to handle them with care.

As if in slow motion, Beres approached her. He had dreamt about this for a week now, about how it was going to be when he met up with her. How everything was going to be all right, how he was going to make things better and do all the things she wanted him to do and buy all the things she wanted, like a new car.

Standing right behind her, he coughed politely.

"Caroline," he said sweetly, "what a surprise."

She spun around.

"Oh..." she said, disappointedly, seeing who it was.

"What a coincidence to see you hear in Tenerife," he soldiered on.

"Yes, isn't it..." she snapped, not giving any ground.

Beres couldn't hide his obvious delight. This was the chance he had been waiting for, to meet her face to face to sort things out. He couldn't have hoped for a better coincidence.

"What are you doing here?" she asked him finally.

"I'm on holiday, with the lads…"

"Out of all the holidays you could have chosen to go on, trust you to choose Tenerife." She kissed her teeth.

"Yes," said Beres brightly.

At the same moment, a bespectacled, handsome, athletic looking black man with a pinstripe moustache and dressed very elegantly in a dark suit, came up and embraced Caroline, then presented her with a beautiful red rose.

"Darling…" he began with a very slight French accent. Then he noticed Beres. "Oh you're the ex, aren't you? You're the guy who gave Caroline up," he said. "I want to thank you." He stretched out his hand. "I'm Jean-Pierre, Caroline's fiancé, I couldn't have done it without you. Thanks."

It was a tricky situation, Beres had no choice but to shake the hand that Jean-Pierre thrust at him. He felt extremely uncomfortable about it.

"I can't believe that you would mess up a relationship with a quality woman like Caroline," the man continued. "I just can't believe it. Quality black women like her are hard to come by, you must have lost your mind. It just goes to show you that there are a lot of foolish black men out there, doesn't it? Anyway, I can't complain, your foolishness is my gain. You can be sure of one thing, I will not make the same mistake as you."

Jean-Pierre turned back to Caroline. "Darling," he said, winking at Beres provocatively as he caressed her bottom, "have I told you today how beautiful you are, how wonderful you are and how much I love you?"

Caroline planted a kiss on his lips. "Oh you are sweet, you say the nicest things... I am so lucky to have finally found the man of my dreams."

"Darling, I can't wait to get you up to our 'honeymoon suite' where we can put up a 'Do Not Disturb' sign while we make some absolutely amazing sex."

Oh, how these Latin lovers love to go over the top compared to your average Afro-Saxon man! Yet Beres kept a stiff upper lip. The couple exchanged a secret smile and Beres felt a shiver go down his spine as he turned a violent shade of purple.

The strain was getting to him, he couldn't take any more. Five minutes of this farce was enough He left the two lovebirds to their smooching and cooing. His parting words to Caroline was that no doubt they would have a chance to sit and talk before the end of the week.

Beres gritted his teeth the whole way back to Las Vinas, steam coming out of his ears as he imagined what Caroline and Jean-Pierre were getting up to right now in their honeymoon suite. Why did she have to rub his face in it? He was prepared to say that he was the one to blame and even take full responsibility for all that had happened between them. As long as he could get credit for the good times, he would take full responsibility for the one bad time he and Caroline had endured together. If she thought that all those good times were worth throwing away for his one (comparatively minor) indiscretion, then there was nothing that he could do about it. But first he needed the opportunity to try and get her to see things from his point of view.

At the end of the day, there was enough fish out in the sea, Beres reassured himself. It wasn't quality black women, but quality black men that there was a real shortage of. Men like himself, who knew how to take care of a sista. Why, he could have his pick of the finest ladies. Maybe Johnny was right after all. Perhaps, with so many single women waiting and hoping that a quality man would come along, it was criminal to be monogamous...

If Beres truly shared Johnny Dollar's views, he might have gone down to the beach to have sex with the first woman that came along. The fact of the matter was that he was a different species from his errant friend and, despite everything that had happened and the humiliation he had had to endure at the hotel, Beres loved Caroline with a passion. Why otherwise would he have spent the rest of that afternoon calling the hotel, trying to get hold of her? He was becoming more and more anxious to talk to her.

He dialled the number again. This time, when the operator put him through to her room, the phone was picked up at the other end.

"Caroline?"

It wasn't. It was Jean-Pierre.

"Beres, oh I'm glad you called. I've been meaning to ask you, tell me again how you let such a quality sista like Caroline slip through your fingers?"

Beres was in no mood for chit-chat. He asked Jean-Pierre to make sure he let Caroline know that he called. He didn't trust him to deliver the message though.

"Is there really any point in passing your message on? After all, you've lost her forever, you know that don't you? There's one thing I can tell you for nothing, you will never find a woman like her anywhere again. Trust me, I know. I've been all over the world looking for a woman like her. I've even hired private detectives to find such a woman, but they never managed to come up with anyone who had her class, her wit, her charm, her intelligence and her... Well, you know how good she is in bed don't you? I still can't believe that you gave that all up for a one night stand. What kind of man are you? That kind of behaviour is old school, or didn't you know? As we go towards the 21st century, brothas can't be acting like that. When we find quality sistas, we stick by them, trust me."

Beres felt stupid. What could he say? He wanted to punch Jean-Pierre in the face. Unfortunately, the telecommunications companies in Japan have not yet invented a telephone which would make that possible from where he was standing. He slammed down the phone instead.

Love and hate could never be friends. Linvall and Marcia's love/hate marriage was volatile to say the least. It was pure 'alms house' business and, to be honest, Gussie and Johnny found it too painful to watch a big old black man like Linvall under heavy manners.

"You're letting Marcia get away with murder," Johnny said. "If you let your woman treat you like that, it won't be long before my woman starts saying, 'Well, if Marcia can get away with it, so can I'."

To his spars, Linvall insisted that he was his own man and that behind closed doors he was master in his own house. If he wanted to, he could still go out and grind any woman on the island and Marcia would have to put up with it.

"The proof of the bullshit is in the eating," Johnny challenged.

For Marcia, it was strange. She had always believed that the longer you dated somebody, the more you should trust them. But their relationship was the opposite, the longer they were together, the less she trusted him. It hadn't always been like that, but she had been duped by him too many times to bring herself to ever trust him again. All she required him to do now was to obey. Pure and simple.

Linvall had been sitting, waiting for her to get ready for what seemed like hours. Whilst Marcia had spent those 'hours' fixing her hair, lamenting that she had hardly brought any clothes with her on this trip (despite the wardrobe full of clothes in her five suitcases), and chatting everybody's business to Lesley, Linvall had occupied his mental faculties with trying to figure out if it was remotely possible that he might still be able to juggle between his wife and any potential holiday romances which might yet manifest themselves.

According to Marcia, she had only accompanied Lesley to Tenerife, so that they could attend a 'Self-Empowerment' weekend being held on the island for followers of Iyanla Vanzant. Linvall knew different. No way had Marcia shelled out a couple of hundred quid to

147

come and listen to a bunch of women talking about how they can become goddesses of the universe. He knew his wife well enough to conclude that she had come to keep an eye on him, to make sure he didn't play away from home.

If only she trusted him more, like every woman should her husband. If only she had a little more faith in him, instead of always interrogating him on where he had been and who he had been with, he might still be able to get a bit on the side from some of the man-hungry women roaming the streets of Tenerife.

Having spent the day taking the 'first lady' sightseeing to Loro Park nature reserve with its beautiful gardens and wildlife, Linvall would have liked some time for himself to make the moves that a man's gotta make. But the 'first lady' aka Marcia, his other half, had insisted that he take her clubbing, "to this Soul Train club that Gussie says you go to every evening. He says it's the best club on the island. It's going to be great going there with you. It will give you a chance to spend some money on me, too."

Linvall's denials that he had ever been to Soul Train and that it was the kind of club Marcia wouldn't see him dead in back home in London, fell on deaf ears. He made a note to throttle Gussie the next time he saw him.

As usual Soul Train was packed with a lot of the regular faces plus many of the holidaymakers who had only landed on the island earlier that day. To Linvall's surprise, many of the regulars were hailing him up like a long time friend as he walked in with his wife. He had been going to the club so regularly now, that he was like part of the furniture. That was his problem. Now, skimpily dressed women were greeting him with sloppy kisses on his cheek. For each kiss, he got a dig in the ribs from Marcia.

"I thought you'd never been to this place," she hissed.

Tenerife was too small an island to go around checking girls and then expecting to keep a low profile. It was even trickier trying to keep a low profile in a crowded club where everybody knew you as a playa. But when a man's gotta go undercover, a man's GOTTA go undercover. Linvall kept disappearing. He told his wife that his bladder was playing up and that he had no choice but to run to the toilets every five minutes, just as she had done when she was pregnant.

Fortunately for him, Marcia was too concerned with doing her *thang* on the dance floor to bother pointing out that Linvall wasn't pregnant. So Linvall was able to maintain a discreet presence.

Even though the ladies in Soul Train were looking particularly *phat* (pretty hot and tempting) tonight, they had no effect on Linvall because of the manners he was under with his wife at the dance. Any other time, he would have been chirpsing to his heart's content but, under these circumstances, it was better for all concerned that he kept his mind off the pretty girls' coconuts.

The last person Linvall was expecting to bump into at Soul Train was Emmanuelle. What was worse was that she seemed to have had a bit too much to drink.

"Hey, big boy!" she greeted him with a slap on the

back. "So how've you been, big boy? Have you missed me, *mon cheri*?" she prickteased.

Aware that the situation could cause a counteraction, Linvall's eyes darted to the left and to the right to make sure that he was not within slapping distance of Marcia.

Emmanuelle threw her arms around his neck and pulled him towards her.

"Memories don't live like peepull do," she sang, "and zey always remember you, whezher sings are good or bad. It's just the memories zat you have…"

Linvall had to admit that she was looking particularly irresistible. Like a Benz or a Bimma. *Zim Zimma!*

"Let me tell you somesink," Emmanuelle purred in his ear. "Understanding women is the key to being a good lover, and what you've got to understand about women is zat we prefer a man wiz a gigantic penis."

Linvall groaned.

"Don't worry, *big* boy," Emmanuelle said. "Every disappointment is for a reason. Maybe when you grow up, you'll get bigger and zen, who knows… Purr-raps Emmanuelle will give you one more chance."

With that she patted him firmly on the crotch. Linvall felt his cock start to get hard. Previous experience was telling him you better leave now because things are happening that ain't supposed to be happening. Unfortunately, it was his brain that was doing the thinking and, as previously established, that was firmly in place in his trousers.

"Come on, *big* boy, buy me a drink," Emmanuelle demanded. "I want the best champagne in the house."

Linvall sneered. It was she who was rich, not him. However, she looked like she might cause a scene if he didn't do as he was told. So he ordered her a glass of the best. It wasn't cheap either.

Past experience was telling him that at this point he should be totally upfront with Emmanuelle, tell her the situation. Tell her that his wife was in the house and liable to box her thirty-two pearly-white teeth out of her mouth if she caught them being overly friendly to one another. At the same time, his cock was telling him, "It nuh finish, it nuh finish, it nuh finish. There is still the possibility of a second grind from this woman. But not tonight."

Linvall made some lame excuse as to why he was in a hurry to get away, and left Emmanuelle with her champagne at the bar.

The cleverest playa could live a thousand years and not come close to figuring women out. No man could ever fully comprehend how dark a woman can be. Little did Linvall know that while Marcia was on the dance floor, she had one eye keeping surveillance on him. Even when her back was turned, she was still watching him...

"So who was that woman you were buying a drink?" she asked him, catching his arm as he tried to slip away.

"Er, what woman?"

Such a wotless question deserved a wotless reply. Marcia conked him hard on the head with her knuckles.

"Oh, *that* woman... She's just a friend."

Marcia laughed out loud.

"Friend! That's what he calls her! You think I'm

simple and you can take me for fool?" This time the conk was even harder. "Linvall, if you want a ride, you get a donkey or a mule, but stop lying."

Emmanuelle appeared out of nowhere to throw in her three francs worth.

"So, Linvall, you're saying zat zis woman is your aunt?"

"No, no," Linvall protested, "I said she was my wife. That's W-I-F..."

When she was a kid, Marcia's seven older brothers nicknamed her 'bonecrusher'. The next thing that happened made Linvall wish that the brothers hadn't also toughened her up as a child.

Kuff-Kuff-Kuff!

The blows came thick and fast and could hardly fail to hit their target as Linvall's nose was as big and broader than Broadway, with cavernous nostrils which had been mistaken for sunglasses on more than one occasion.

"You should honour your baby mother, not disrespect her," Marcia explained, rubbing her knuckles. " 'Cause your baby mother is the best thing in your life."

As Linvall tended to his nose, an English guy who had seen the commotion came up to them.

"Instead of you two having a fight, why don't you come to my pub across the road. Two drinks for the price of one. It's happy hour all night long."

He tried to hand Marcia a leaflet, but it wasn't her 'happy hour'. She sized him up menacingly and told him in no uncertain terms: "MOVE!" Then, for no particular reason, she decided to give Linvall two more licks.

Kuff-kuff.

Gussie arrived at Soul Train just in time to help Linvall to his feet. Seeing Emmanuelle and Marcia standing over his friend, Gussie made a quick and accurate assessment of the situation.

He grinned at Linvall. "So much for 'I can grind any woman on the island if I want to'."

Linvall's anger boiled inside. Gussie was as good a scapegoat as any to turn his venom on. It was Gussie who had got him into this mess in the first place. When he thought about it, Gussie had been getting him into messes all throughout the holiday. Well, he thought, every barrow-hog has his saturday to go to slaughter. This was far from over, or, in the Jamaican patois he often switched to at times of anger and despair, "It nuh finish, it nuh finish it nuh finish."

ISMS 'N' SCHISMS

Linvall having dragged his sorry backside home to Las Vinas, Gussie was left to savour the best of the talent in Soul Train. Staying well away from Emmanuelle he started 'wining' with one gal in the corner. He was happily wining away, when he felt a tap on his shoulder. He ignored it. Wining this good needed your full concentration. He felt the tap again, this time it was harder. He looked round and almost jumped back in shock as he came face to face with TV personality Angela Braithwaite, the woman who he had donated his sperm to.

"A-A-A-A-A-A-Angela..." Gussie stuttered.

"Pull yourself together, tell that little gal bye-bye, and take me back to my hotel. I need to talk to you," Angela said very officiously.

"A-A-A-A-A-A-Angela..." Gussie spluttered again.

In the taxi going back to her hotel, Gussie found out that the BBC had sent Angela to Tenerife to do a holiday programme from the island. Three days of filming in the sun. The last person she expected to bump into was the surrogate father for her children. But it was just as well, she said, because there were very pressing matters that needed to be sorted out between them before the babies were born.

This totally confused Gussie. What did it have to do with him now? Wasn't she the one who didn't want him to have anything to do with the children? Wasn't it she who made him sign a contract relinquishing all the rights to the children before she would pay him his surrogacy fee?

Yes, she said. That was all true. But the circumstances were different. She had paid him a fee to be the surrogate father to her child, not her children. How was she to know that she was going to end up having twins? If Gussie had bothered to read the itsybitsy teenyweeny small print, he would have known that the contract was only valid for the birth of one child. Why should she pay for feeding, clothing and shelter for two kids for the next eighteen years when she could only afford one? The second child, would be Gussie's responsibility. Oh, she would raise the child with its twin but, and here was the bit she wanted Gussie to pay special attention to, he would pay for that second child.

"If you're the gentleman I think you are, you'll provide for that child to have the best of everything — a five bedroom house in the suburbs set in an acre or two of land, a private nanny, the best education at one of the country's top private schools and three Caribbean holidays a year."

Gussie wanted to say, 'I'm not a gentleman, I'm a playa, and if you make such a wotless suggestion again, I'll kick your frigging arse. Most definitely'. But he didn't. He had a set of twins on the way and, deep down, he would do anything he could to help them. But he didn't have the cash.

"Of course, if you're not a gentleman, I can always give the Child Support Agency your name and address. I believe that they have ways of turning errant fathers into gentlemen."

All Gussie could think about was 'under manners'! Now he knew what it meant to be under heavy manners. Now he knew what poor Linvall had to live with. The pickney hadn't even arrived yet and Angela was already threatening him with the CSA! At this rate it wouldn't be long before she was considering committing cold-blooded murder.

The self-empowerment workshop was entitled 'Black Women Mean Business' and was being held at the Hotel Sierra by Yoruba High Priestess Mamoniya Olafemi aka Annie Jackson from the Stonebridge Estate, Harlesden, a devotee of Iyanla Vanzant. It was Annie's great idea to have the workshop in Tenerife.

Many sistas find these get-togethers a reassuring time to share and understand the female experience. When sistas come together there is no need to be formal. The atmosphere is relaxed and the participants can forget convention, for a while at least.

After having gone through various breathing exercises and offering libations up to the Goddess, Annie had led the group in a twenty minute meditation on the female ancestors who had gone before.

Then it was down to business.

For the next three hours the twenty sistas-in-spirit, all sporting African headwraps, sat together in the hotel's conference room discussing the way forward. Annie tried to steer them towards doing it for themselves. Taking the bull by the horn, and leaving their secretarial jobs, leaving their wotless partners and starting that business they had been thinking about for years. The rest of the women, on the other hand, just wanted to discuss relationships. To Annie's frustration

Annie was from the old school and her philosophy was that men had only two faults: Everything they say and everything they do.

"If you want to better yourself, there's no point in hanging around for your man to come correct," she argued. "Look how long we've been waiting so far? May I remind you of all the things men have put you through? Can you really be the woman you want to be with the man you know? The answer is clearly 'No'. Sistas, you should be leaving the past behind and stepping into the future. In the future, black men will no longer be relevant. Single life for a black woman in the twenty-first century is going to be exciting, refreshing, profitable and positively better than it has been in the nineties. In the twenty-first century, we can be ourselves. No more panicking if marriage isn't on the horizon by the time we hit twenty. No more rushing to the altar with the first idiot we bump into. The twenty-first century black woman will be over-qualified, over-paid and single."

Some of the sistas derived strength from the fact that they were single because they had left relationships that weren't working, and now had time to consider their own requirements.

Sista Ntozake Bimbola (Hortense McCalla) said that she had been single for a year with a daughter from her last relationship. "I had been jumping from one passionate relationship to the other, hoping to find happiness. But now I realise so much about myself, about what I need. I was dating all these good looking men with nothing between their ears, who were so wrong for me. I was lost but now I am found. Time has taught me that I don't need a man. You get used to the lack of sex. It would be nice, but then, if you just want that you can get it anywhere, can't you? I tell myself every day: I DON'T NEED A MAN, I DON'T NEED A MAN, I DON'T NEED A MAN. I don't need a man to make love to me, I don't even need a man to talk to on those lonely nights when all you can think of is how all the other women in the neighbourhood are bonking happily away with their men, while your upstairs neighbour is getting through a really thorough sexual workout with her new man and the moans of passion are floating up from your downstairs neighbour as her man pushes it slowly in and out and in and out and in and out and in and out and..."

"Yes, yes, yes. I think we get the point," Annie interrupted.

"But you see what I mean," Hortense gasped, her hands between her legs, "I... don't uh-uh... need... ugggghhhhhnnnnn a... mmmmmnnn... black man... What *(yesssss!)* I miss the most *(oooooohhh yeeeeeessssss!)* is the feeling that someone loves you, the intimacy *(YES! YESSS!! YEEEEEESSSSSSSSSS!!!!!)*"

"All right, that's quite enough, thank you," Annie

came in for the second time.

Some of the other sistas weren't altogether convinced that anything men could do, they could do better. For example, brothas seemed to have the edge when it came to wotlessness. Besides, these sistas only came on this trip so that they could check the most amount of men and, hopefully, get one to church on time. They certainly weren't ready to contemplate a life without men.

"What's a girl to do in the meantime?" asked Grace Mango (for that was her real name), a mini mampie. "Exactly how do you cope without a man? Hug your pillow, your teddy bear or your cat night after night? Boy, you women must be lonely, guy. Sex is a biological need, a natural craving. It's also one thing that you can't replace. It's a need that begs to be satisfied. How can people not want sex? Like the song says, birds do it, bees do it, why shouldn't I an' I do it?"

"There is an alternative," Annie said. "Masturbation is a good one, whether people want to talk about it or not. There are umpteen sex toys on the market. It's safe and offers you a chance to get to know what your body really needs in lovemaking. You'll find that that's not a man."

Princess Ashika Nefertiti (aka Millicent Martin), a thirty-three year old single mother who divorced eighteen months previously spoke next.

"I married the first guy that really asked me out. Back then I was doe-eyed and innocent. We went steady all through college and got married in our final year. He got a degree, I went into labour. After eleven years of marriage, I realized how much time I had wasted with him and wanted to be on my own. So there I was, a single woman of the nineties. A friend had given me a bouquet of roses to celebrate my freedom, so on impulse I scattered the petals across my nice new sheets in my own apartment and dived on top of them. It was the best feeling in the world. At first, all the responsibility was terrifying as I'd been married since I was twenty-two. But when I discovered that I was a princess of the universe, I started finding my feet. I feel that my true personality is being expressed for the first time. I go where I want to go, I see who I want to see when I am ready. I have a lot more time for my work and I am now a successful businesswoman, I have a home in an exclusive neighbourhood and a lovely son. Why do I need a man? Except, perhaps, to have another child."

A round of applause led by Annie rang out in the conference room.

"You see," Annie continued, "our priorities are misplaced. People think that you have to have a man to become a valid person. Princess Ashika is living proof that there is a life without men. Maybe it's because I've never been in love, but a large part of me can't relate to all that hearts and flowers thing, not to mention the friends I have who are in destructive relationships just because they 'need' a man. What for? To feel better about themselves? I feel fine about myself already. My mother is having a nervous breakdown about it, but she's just going to have to live with it just like I have to live with her subtle and not so subtle hints about finding a man, settling down and producing grandchildren, every time I visit her. When I say I like being single, I can feel people thinking that it's weird that I've never been with a man. They wonder what's wrong with me, don't I want a bonk, am I a lesbian? This is the way I want to live my life because this is the best way to live my life."

Sista Afemi Malinga aka Barbara Smith, sporting a particularly multi-coloured headwrap, agreed with Annie. The two men in her life had both been 'dogs' — her husband and her father.

"Men will always let you down, there's nothing that can be done about it," she said. "All men are dogs. If you lie with dogs you must rise with fleas, or at least genital lice. So don't trust them, y'hear sistas? Why share your life with a dog? Why compromise your independence with one? Dyam dog bit me already. Once bitten twice shy. Believe me, sistas, that dog's biting days are over, I made sure of that. Can't bite if you don't have teeth. You know what I mean sistas?" Barbara said with a sly wink.

Grace Mango was still not convinced and once again aired her dissatisfaction about being single.

"Well, if you all aren't checking men on this trip, there'll be more for me," she said, getting up. "I don't care what any of you say, woman can not live without man. I'm off to find a man to love me and hug me and squeeze me on those lonely nights when you're all meditating. I want a husband, I don't want to be single no more."

Sista Shabazz Nurridin (Lesley Lindo) could keep silent no longer. Her soul was hurting deep within. She got up to speak.

"Sista Grace, fools die for want of wisdom. Believe, me I know. I nearly died in my relationship with the 'original baby father'. Every time I turned my head, it seemed he was producing another child by yet another woman. I was demoralized, I didn't know what to do. My life had lost direction. I became quite jealous when I saw relationships that were obviously working. But for every one of those, I saw a thousand that weren't. So I decided to go solo a week ago, and since then my life has been blissful. Even if you're in love with someone, I mean if you're REALLY in love with someone, the last thing you want to do is make the mistake of marrying them."

"You hear that Sista Grace?" said Annie. Then reverting to her native patois, "If you nuh hear, you bettah beware!"

Funny how women can spot another woman's hair on your jacket, yet miss the garage doors when they're parking a car, Beres pondered as he sat down to dinner. He was wearing the tie that Caroline had bought him because she said he looked cute in it, the one with the Mickey Mouse motif. She hadn't even noticed.

"This is no laughing matter," she snapped when Beres said how delighted he was to see her and that, like Hughie Green, he meant that most sincerely, folks!

Beres had finally managed to get hold of Caroline and had literally begged to have a meeting with her, that there were important things to be discussed. He promised that it would be strictly business. It was an untruth of course, but he had to get close to her by hook or by crook. After all, these were very early days yet, Caroline and Jean-Pierre had only been lovers for a matter of weeks. Beres could still save his marriage with some serious let's-get-back-together-again lyrics and a lot of good fortune. Beres knew, better than Jean-Pierre, what Caroline's weaknesses were. He remembered that she got horny any time someone touched her neck. He also knew that she couldn't resist going horse riding. He had taken the liberty of hiring a couple of horses from the local riding school for the next day.

When Caroline agreed to the meeting, Beres felt so bubbly and cheerful that he offered to take her to the best restaurant on the island and even offered to pay. Caroline said that was fine and then mentioned ("Oh, by the way...") that Jean-Pierre would be coming along for the ride.

Beres took a deep breath. I can handle this, he told himself. I will be nice.

Beres was so nervous about the meeting that he coached himself for several hours beforehand. He now knew how to maintain a plastic smile on his face when the urge to throttle Jean-Pierre overcame him, as it did the moment he arrived. Jean-Pierre's habit of peering over his prescription spectacles puppy-dog style when he spoke, made Beres want to give him a hard slap.

The restaurant, was up in the hills overlooking the bay at Las Caletas. It was owned by an elderly Dutch guy and was frequented by the likes of Michael Jackson whenever he was on the island. They certainly had the most expensive wine Beres had ever seen on a menu, and it seemed like Caroline was determined to rinse out his money.

As he thought about how he went home and bawled his eyes out after Caroline revealed on the *Janet Sinclair Show* that she was leaving him, Beres kept a moronic smile on his face. Jean-Pierre had no choice but to smile back. It was then that Beres noticed the tiny diamond set into one of Jean Pierre's front teeth. Jean-Pierre was obviously big banking. That was one more reason for Beres to slap him. One thing was for sure, Beres was not going to pay for Jean-Pierre's meal. No way.

"Fancy going horse riding tomorrow, Caroline?" Beres asked

She simply kissed her teeth.

"Hey Caroline, you've got something on your neck. Let me remove it."

Jean Pierre was too quick and held Beres' hand in a tight grip before he was able to lay a finger on her.

"Caroline already has a man who is capable of doing any plucking that's needed.

"So what did you want to talk about," said Caroline as she and Jean-Pierre ordered two portions each of the most expensive meals on the menu.

Beres began slowly, hesitantly, conscious that Jean-Pierre was lapping up every word of it. He felt awkward, like an outsider in his own home. He had a frown on his face, but his style wasn't to argue with his wife in front of another man, even if it was her fiancé, especially if it was her fiancé. He explained, as best he could how he felt that Caroline's unruly son had been a particular strain on him in their relationship. Caroline was too protective over him and had forbidden Beres to flog him even if he was outta order.

"No disrespect, Caroline, I'm just saying that it was difficult, he will never see me as his father. I'm sure you can sympathise to a certain extent, because you've had to put up with my daughter. Dating someone with offspring can be fraught, a potential minefield of embarrassment, resentment or open hostility. Nevertheless I think we can make our relationship work. Maybe we could send your son to boarding school or something."

"Is that it?" asked Caroline, after insisting that Jean-Pierre tuck into the most expensive dessert on the menu, though she wouldn't as she wanted to stay nice and trim.

No, it was not it. Beres wanted to tell her that despite the fact that she wasn't the same person after they got married and were unable to agree on even watching the same TV programme, that he still loved her.

"I'm just crazy about you," he stated. "I can't help myself."

He looked at her hard and considered. But he couldn't guess what she was thinking. Then he looked at Jean-Pierre who made no attempt to hide the fact that he was only there for a free meal.

"Furthermore," Beres continued, "I don't like to point out that, with over sixty percent of all black couples divorcing, buppies like you and I ought to be setting a better example and working through our relationships and coming to a mutual understanding without having to separate."

Caroline nodded her head as she thought about what Beres had said for a full minute. Just as he thought she was coming around to his way of reasoning, she finally opened her mouth. She decided to break it to him gently.

"I don't think I'll ever feel as much for you as I do for Jean-Pierre. I have almost forgotten what you look like. Beres, you have not been forgiven, but you have been forgotten."

Quietly, but purposefully, she told Beres that he was a bastard. Beres felt a shiver running up his spine.

"When we got married, we swore that we would be faithful to one another. I stood there in front of all my friends and gave my heart to you. And all because you couldn't resist the next woman who opened her legs for you, you decided to throw it all away. Even my friends have been telling me I deserve to be treated better than that."

"You do," Beres conceded.

"You don't have to tell me I do, I already know," she snapped. "And now I've got someone who treats me better." She slipped her arm around Jean-Pierre. "My relationship with him is secure. We don't have to play games He gives me something you are not able to. I've got the perfect guy."

"Hey, Beres, never mind," Jean-Pierre chipped in, "you've lost Caroline for good, but here," he handed Beres a slip of paper. "Those are the number of a couple of women that were after me for ages before you handed Caroline to me on a platter. Call them up. I don't happen to find them attractive, but you might."

Baby Father 3: *Does my batty look big in this?*

Beres didn't know what else to say so he said, "Caroline, I'm sorry, I will make it up to you."

He was running out of time. He had to get rid of Jean-Pierre or face the prospect of someone else being married to the woman he should still be married to.

He said he needed to go to the toilet but, instead, slipped out of the restaurant leaving his rival to pay for the extremely expensive meal.

Johnny couldn't believe that Lesley wouldn't give him enough rope to hang himself. He had gone next door on his hands and knees. But Lesley (or Sista Shabazz Nurridin as she now preferred to be refered to) wasn't interested in what he had to say and told him so repeatedly. She was too wise for that. Too wise, too old, too long in the tooth. When it came to Johnny she had him sussed — inside out. As far as she was concerned his mouth was full up of lies, not promises. She hated the sight of him.

He had never seen her this militant, this uncompromising, or was it false pride? If he had bothered to read the book that she had flung in his face, he might have understood a little better where she was coming from. But he wasn't interested in Iyanla Vanzant, or meditations for women of colour.

"You must take me for some kind of fool if you think I'm even going to listen to another word you've got to say," she told him before slamming the door on his nose.

"Oh please come back to me," Johnny wailed, "can't you see, I need you desperately!"

She was going to settle for nothing less than fifty percent of everything Beres earned. Angela Braithwaite wasn't ramping. Beres realized that when she flung a paperback book in his face and told him to "Read that."

The book was entitled *The Baby Father's Guide* and it was by Patrick Augustus. Beres sat down and started reading:

Part of being a baby father is looking after your woman/mother of the child. She's just told you that she's pregnant, so:

Don't let her lift up anything too heavy, she needs plenty of rest.

She needs to be sitting down and resting quite a bit. Miscarriage is possible, so don't run go buy her a bottle of wine. She has to do without alcohol from now on.

You may be surprised at the different reactions from your bonafide spars when you tell them the news:

"She's trapped you. She mussa tie you down wid rice an' peas."

"She don't look like marriage material to me, why did you go and do a stupid thing like that?"

"You lucky son of a gun..."

Baby Father 3: *Does my batty look big in this?*

"Congratulations. Maybe that child will one day discover a cure for cancer/AIDS."

"You're gonna have to be responsible now."

Now that you're about to become a baby father, you need to carry a condom around at all times. Remember, if you decide to play away from home, your child could be harmed by all sorts of venereal diseases. So, you need to saddle up!

Cut down the evenings out with the boys from seven times a week to (at the most) five times a week — especially if there's no one else around to help.

At this point you may find that you have to consider marriage in the old fashioned way. But don't worry, being a divorcee isn't as bad as it sounds.

All you should be concerned about is that there are no complications with the pregnancy and that the baby is born healthy and that the mother survives. Meanwhile, you can't feel no way when your baby mother asks you to run go to the petrol station late at night to buy her some ice cream and spaghetti. Even though you're thinking, 'No wonder she's been so bloody sick'.

A lot of men think that women are really looking attention when they say they're sick with morning sickness — most of the time it's genuine.

Now, one important thing to remember about all of this:

Patrick Augustus

It's just called morning sickness, but it can occur all day long.

You'll also be expected to accompany your baby mother for regular scans at the hospital, where you'll be able to see the baby for the first time, hear its heart beating, and find out how fast it's growing. If it's big for its age, it's probably going to be premature. You can even find out if it's going to be a boy or girl. Oh, you'll find out how your partner's blood pressure is also.

Women love it when you accompany them to ante-natal classes because they don't want everybody assuming that they haven't got a father for the child. At least they want people to see that the father cares and it's not just another ghetto bastard. At least they can keep up appearances if you show a willingness to be by their side.

At ante-natal classes, they teach you how to help your partner in labour with breathing exercises. Try to remember, it's about her breathing, not yours. At ante-natal classes, the midwife will tell you as much as possible about all the different experiences you're about to go through, and offload a whole heap of leaflets telling you the same thing again. All men will agree that these classes are very boring, but it is advisable not to start checking your watch every five minutes to see if you can still make your runnings, because you're liable to get a response such as this from your baby mother: "I've been asking you to come along to these classes for weeks and now you're here, all you want to do is rush away. You can't even sacrifice two hours of your precious time for your baby!" Basically don't rush. Two hours is a small price to pay for your baby mother's happiness. Besides, at ante-natal classes you'll see how other men behave with their baby mothers. Let that be a lesson to you.

As a prospective baby father you should read up baby books and speak to other people who have had kids before and start watching TV programmes on kids, especially those on cot deaths and breastfeeding (though, do not attempt to try the latter yourself!)

Things that will now be going through your mind:

If it's your first time, you might be over the moon, even though you don't know what you're letting yourself in for. A lot of men think they'll be able to handle it. Ignorance is bliss. You have to knock your old ways on the head, because you'll be broke from now on. Those freebies you used to do for people has to come to an end. Although there will be certain people you still want to give a squeeze, you will have to start getting serious with cash and start economising. There will be another mouth to feed in nine months time, so start preparing for it now. Everything to do with babies is expensive — a pram can set you back £300, disposable nappies and baby food are expensive... baby everything is expensive.

At this point you may also start thinking of names. Will you christen your child with a name that's got meaning or will your child's name be the perpetuation of another slavemaster's name?

Now that your baby's here and you have a son/daughter and heir, who will inherit all your worldly goods:

Maybe it's time to consider a will. Don't be like the late reggae king Bob Marley and die intestate, 'cause you nevah know who's going to get their hands on your money when you're gone. As the Bible says, it might be someone who doesn't deserve it.

Avoid bottled milk at this stage. The child wants to be breastfed (especially boys). That is another reason to be on good terms with the baby mother, for she is the only source for the perfect nourishment for your baby. Breastfeeding should stop at twelve months. Some kids are still being breastfed at five years old. This madness has got to stop.

Many mothers allow their babies to sleep in the king size bed with mummy and daddy to begin with, then when it's time for the cot the child is wary and refuses. My good spar Donald's kid has had a brand new cot standing there for five months and not one night has the kid spent in it. Babies must sleep in their own bed from day one!

My kids could all sleep through hoovering, TV, anything. I don't know if that's hereditary... I didn't change my lifestyle to accommodate them. However, most babies wake at the slightest noise. So tiptoe through the tulips.

Seeing the beautiful bouncing toddler, you start imagining what your baby's going to become when s/he becomes older. At this point, all baby fathers are optimistic and confident that their child will become a doctor, lawyer, footballer. But flogging your children to become what you want to become is

172

old school. That belongs to our parent's generation. Nowadays you have to consider the child first and what s/he wants to do and just support them. Pay for music lessons, ballet lessons, football lessons, take them to museums. Most importantly, pay for a back-up education(Saturday school, private home tuition every evening etc). Do not rely on state education unless you live in an area of great affluence. Give your children a range of things to choose from.

You may even be thinking about an arranged marriage already. When I first became a baby father, I used to spend a lot of time looking at other babies in their prams and thinking, 'Yeah, that one's going to be a suitable partner for my daughter when he grows up. If you meet other kids from a good family, make them know each other from now.

A good baby father will trust his baby mother to be faithful and loyal. Try your very best to behave in that way also:

Allow your partner to have her own space and try to assist her in what she wants to do. Now that she's pregnant, she may have a penchant for studying law, it will be a good idea to buy her a book on that subject. If your partner is subsequently successful in her studies and has a higher status than yourself, do not think negative and believe that her success highlights your failure.

If you and your partner have a problem, try to sort it out before you go to bed. Very often, two people go to bed and only one wakes up, by this time it's too late to say 'sorry'.

It's important to remember that bringing up a child is a full time job — by no means easy. So, it would be nice if you could help out with the domestic work. I am quite sure she would love breakfast in bed once in a while.

Look after each other. You may not even have to spend much cash to do this. You'll be surprised to know that some baby mothers are happy enough just walking in the local park hand in hand and talking. It is vital to your relationship that the communication does not break down. Your partner may develop a new interest and you ought to know about it, sooner rather than later. After a hard day's work, a massage would go down well. Occasionally, go out to dinner and remember, what it took to get her pregnant is what it will take to keep her.

Now that your pickney is growing up:

Try to attend parent evenings at the nursery. Keep in contact with the teachers. If they see you take an interest in your child, they will also. At weekends, try and do something interesting and educational with the family. Take baby mother and child to a museum, the zoo etc.

Now that your child is a walking, talking five year old, always ask your child how his/her day has been and what s/he learned at school. Did something happen at school that you should know about?

How you control one child may not be the same as how you

control another. Beating your child when s/he is rude, is not the only control mechanism one can use. According to the age of the child, there are other methods.

You can start teaching your child as young as five months manners and respect. My son, for example, kept on spitting at five months and I had to stop him. He knows not to do it now. Of course, different children have varying intelligence.

You may be worried that despite having taught your child well, you can see that s/he hasn't been paying attention. Who don't hear must feel.

If a child is 2-4 years old and you've told him/her not to play with matches on more than one occasions and s/he's still flicking matches about the place, a wringing of the ears is necessary. If the child swears or spits (especially at adults) and has no respect or manners, that will call for some old time licks. Proper licks, for which you may need a big stick. Again, for teefing, proper licks is required, as with unnecessary rudeness to nursery school teachers after several warnings. When communication between you and your child breaks down, turn to that passage in the Bible which says, "spare the rod and spoil the child."

If the child is between 5-16 years old, send him/her to the confines of his/her room after dinner. Take away all privileges. Find out what your child's hobbies are and deprive him/her of it.

Make them miss their favourite TV programmes or ban them from going to the next birthday party that comes up, or stop them going to the cinema, a dance, or the weekend football match. Alternatively, make him/her stand on a chair in the centre of the room without moving for a whole day and, even though s/he whines and whines and whines, don't relent. When all else fails, a good old fashioned flogging always does the trick, though may not stand up in court.

If the child is sixteen years old or over s/he probably won't care, in which case, you have to give him/her some rahtid hard work to do, like making sure s/he does all the gardening, cleans the house and does the shopping. Throw some lines and essays on top and enforce a curfew. If s/he's still rude don't allow him/her to buy his/her own designer label clothes, instead make sure that they go to school in some extremely conservative Marks & Spencer clothes which you have chosen. Most youts won't want to go to school like that, but if they don't behave they have to get used to being the odd one out at school with a duffel coat instead of a criss blazer. If s/he's still rude call up your local authority and find out from what age you can legally kick him/her out. I wouldn't recommend t'umping a yout' of this age because s/he might t'ump you back.

A good baby father is one who sets a good example for his children to be proud of and follow. Teach your child respect and manners through your example.

Be very careful what you expose them to. Don't leave your pornographic videos about the place, giving them access to t'ings they're not supposed to see and picking up language dem nah fe pick up. Don't swear at or fight your baby mother in front of them. Try not to swear or do anything you do not want your children to do. Children are very impressionable and their biggest influence is their parents. Show them by example the importance of reading, by making sure you read a lot of good books also. Me, personally, I read the Bible with my pickney and make them see where my principles are coming from. I show them, through Marcus Garvey and other great works for humanity, where they're coming from.

Like my nephew, Patrice, he's ten years old and quite intelligent — or so he will tell you. He's a problem for his grandmother because she's not as educated as he is, and he will deliberately embarrass her by drawing on big words so that she doesn't know what he's saying. The moral of that story is that every baby father and baby mother should keep up with their education, because your child is just itching for the day when s/he is able to embarrass you intellectually. One good thing about Patrice is that he knows where he's coming from, and when he goes to school he lets the teachers know, in no uncertain terms, that 'I will not let you or your education brainwash me'. But he loves his pocket money and saves every penny of it because he wants to go into business like his father. So if he doesn't do what you tell him to, you have to withdraw his allowance. So now, we just give his pocket money to his teachers and, you know what, he's not so cheeky in class and he's top in every subject.

You can avoid a lot of illnesses by providing a good, healthy balanced diet for your children daily. If possible cut down on meats, sugar, salt, dairy products. Read up on it. A lot of adults today blame their parents for their bad eating habits and frequent visits to the dentist or doctor. Think of your high *blood pressure.*

EVERY baby father should take an interest in ALL of his children's welfare (i.e. physically, emotionally, culturally, spiritually etc). You should be involved in all major decisions with each baby mother concerning each child's wants and needs.

You should show the world and society that you have legal and personal PR (parental responsibility) over your children.

EVERY baby father should spend quality time with their children with consistency. If you have an honest and sincere relationship with your children, it allows the children to confide in you and freely express themselves — a friendship relationship.

I know it is sometimes difficult, but bite your tongue and try to maintain a friendly relationship with the baby mother. Her welfare, health and strength is vital to the success of your children. To hurt your baby mother is to hurt your child.

Choose the right time and place to introduce your children to their half siblings. Whenever possible, bring all your children together.

Do not try to turn your children against their mother even if the mother tries to turn them against you. It's good if the children's mother and father can be seen by the children to have a meal together every now and then.

Baby Father 3: *Does my batty look big in this?*

A good baby father will know he is a good baby father, because he will constantly hear that from the baby mother who, despite differences, says he is a good baby father. The good baby father's children are always happy to see and be with him. The fact that his children are never afraid of him and have never seen the hostile side of him, even though its there, is a good quality. A good baby father is one who would fight to see or have access to his children and insist on being responsible for them even if it means going to court.

Do not leave it up to the welfare state to care for your children.

A good baby father is one who knows that he owes his children while his children don't owe him.

But dis nuh finish, it nuh finish, it nuh finish...

BOOM-SHAK-A-LAK

"Greetings, in the name of the Most High — King of Kings, Lord of Lords, Conquering Lion of the Tribe of Judah, elect of God, ever living God, earth's rightful ruler. Selassie-I!"

If Johnny didn't know better he would have sworn that the man was a spitting image of Patrick Augustus. But Napthali was white. Or so Johnny believed. He was in fact a Canary Islander — born and grown, and hated the Spanish who had colonized his island with a passion. But more importantly for Johnny's purpose, he was the local herb vendor.

The man spread out a mat and went into his cave and came out carrying a crocus bag filled to the brim with what must have been the most amount of ganja that Johnny had ever seen. All different types of ganja — sensi, lamb's bread, indica, skunk, hash, bush herb. There must have been at least four or five ki's of weed there.

"Bredrin, welcome to the ganja exchange. Me have ganja, an' me have the real sensimilla. Oh bumboclaat, oh raas claat! Good sensimilla to make you prosper longer, 'cause when t'ings an' times was really slow, strictly ganja mek the money flow fe I an' I right yah so inna Tenerife. Although it may sound funny, ganja brings in the good tourist money."

Apart from some skunk that someone had brought in from Holland, most of the weed in Tenerife was from Senegal. Like an expert wine taster, Johnny could tell his boss weed from his bush herb. All he had to do was smell it to know whether it was a particularly good vintage. 1998, for example, was proving to be a particularly successful harvest for sensi smokers.

Johnny made the mistake of suggesting that Napthali's weed was just average.

"Oh bumbo claat, oh raas claat! Bredrin, if it's good enough for the rastas in Jamaica, it's good enough for you," the white rasta declared. "This is the very same weed that was found on King Solomon's grave — the weed of wisdom."

The devil finds work for idle hands, and having had no sex for some time, Johnny turned his mind to the next best thing — a good stick of weed. But in the short time he had been on the island, he had, regretfully, come to the conclusion that it was very rare to get a proper draw in Tenerife. This fact had been brought home to him outside Soul Train when he rolled up the few crumbs of weed he had found at the bottom of his suitcase from a previous holiday. As the sweet and distinct aroma of a lit spliff floated out in the evening air, Johnny became like a Pied Piper with a long line of dopeheads on his trail.

One gal came up to him and said, "Have you got a spliff?" Johnny kissed his teeth at her. For one thing, he hadn't even tasted the spliff yet and, furthermore, it was all the spliff he possessed on this godforsaken island, the last thing he was going to do was share it with a complete stranger. Even when the gal made it quite clear that the trade off was 'sex for ganja' ("Like 'arms for Iraq' or the Iran-Contra deal, only with balls," she offered), Johnny still declined.

"Excuse me while I light my spliff," he told her. "And, no, you can't have any of it. So, settle an' cool..." To begin with, he didn't check pork. Moreover, when it came to sex or a man's last spliff, those few crumbs from the bottom of his suitcase had the edge — every time.

After the buzz he got from that spliff, Johnny was just coming to terms with spending the rest of his holiday without another decent draw, when an African street vendor he got into conversation with informed him that he could get a decent draw from Napti, the weed vendor. Value for money spliffs compared to the street price.

Only after Johnny had parted with a portion of money for a watch he didn't want, did the vendor agree to take him to Las Caletas to the east of Playa de Las Americas, where Napthali lived with a dozen others in what Britain's tabloid papers would have described as, an encampment of new age travellers/white rastas/eco warriors/anarchists/anti-establishment middle class students living rough/trustafarians. Some were locksmen, others baldhead rastas, punky dreads, funki dreds, some had their hair in beaded plaits and top-knots — white dreadlocks in the making.

It was a long walk to get to the settlement, the last leg of which was compounded by a steep hill which Johnny was finding arduous to climb. At the summit, a spectacular view awaited them of a completely secluded bay at which the ocean continually lashed out with its powerful waves. Carved into the cliff were several caves each of which now housed a family of the said social outcasts, all of whom sported a caucasian version of the natty dreadlock style once fashioned on the streets of Trenchtown, Jamaica, by the likes of Bob Marley, Peter Tosh, Bunny Wailer, Big Youth and others too numerous to mention.

When Johnny first saw Napthali, he was standing outside his cave looking out to sea contemplatively. He was barechested beneath a waistcoat and wearing army camouflage trousers, kung fu shoes and a red green and gold scarf tied around his long mane of black straggly locks. With a spliff in one hand and a Heineken in the other, he greeted Johnny Dollar with a smile that revealed a mouth full of gold teeth. Apart from the teeth and the fact that he was white (at least Johnny assumed he was white), he could have earned a living as a stunt double for Patrick Augustus.

Napthali had apparently learnt his English from old Studio One records, and he now had an irritating habit of answering every question with a line from a Burning Spear song or some other reggae classic.

"Do you remember the bumboclaat days of slavery?" Napthali retorted, when Johnny asked him whether he was prepared to barter a little on the price of a good spliff. And when Johnny mentioned that he was a bit low on Rizlas and asked Napthali if he could tell him where he might purchase some, Napthali replied, "When I was a yout' I used to bu'n colly weed in a rizla, now me come a man me jus' ah bu'n sensimilla in a chalwa. Legalize it, and I will advertise it... oh what a raas claat!"

Apparently, Napthali was also the president of the local chapter of the Legalize Cannabis campaign. They were planning a march through Playa de Las Americas to challenge recent government claims that excessive use of cannabis can lead to short term memory, only Napthali couldn't remember when the demonstration was to take place.

Napthali insisted that Johnny stayed to smoke a peace pipe with him. "Smoking the pipe is like flying," he explained. "Smoking a spliff is just cruising, but if you want to fly, you've got to bu'n the chalice inna bumboclaat Buckingham Palace."

It was the most powerful weed Johnny had ever smoked, hot like fire he nearly dropped the chalice. Just one lick of it and his head was buzzing like crazy. He could feel it in his blood, in his bones and in his toes. He could feel it right up to his brain. Just one puff and his eyes were popping out of their sockets and his body shut down like he was paralyzed. He expressed his approval with a faint nod of the head. That was all he could manage, then he passed the pipe to Napti.

Napthali disappeared behind a cloud of thick white smoke, as he burned up the rest of the weed at the bottom of the coconut shell chalice with one long inhalation.

"You see me," Napthali's voice came through the haze, "I-man ah de bush doctor, an' me seh ganja is a cure for asthma, glaucoma an' plenty other dangerous diseases, like the one called the elephantitis, the other one is the poliomyelitis, arthritis and the one diabetes. Oh bumboclaat, oh raas claat, the amount of doctors, lawyers an' players of instruments who smoke it. I-man ah de minister, a mystic man — an intelligent diplomat for His Imperial Majesty. I don't drink no champagne, an' I-man don't sniff no cocaine. Strictly vegetarian, I don't eat up no fried chicken, nor hamburgers or frankfurters. I don't drink no pink, green, nor raas claat yellow soda pop. I-man don't play fool's games on saturdays. I-man don't fornicate on a sunday. I an' I just come to flash lightning, earthquake and thunder in these places of destruction and worthiness, that's why babylon ah fight I an' I so hard fe a stick of weed. Don't they know that this herb was found on Solomon's grave. This herb is for the use of man. This island is African land where the herb has been growing for thousands of years. We make our shoes and socks and clothes out of the herb as well. It's strong, tough like rope, y'know. Everybody all over the world wants the herb to be free, so I and I don't observe the Spanish law because I and I is African, seen? Oh what a bumboclaat, oh what a raas claat…"

The weed was obviously affecting Napthali big time. Johnny was still incapacitated and had no choice but to listen to the white rasta's brimstone and fire philosophy.

"See how long these pirates like Christopher Columbus have been robbing, raping and kidnapping my African people," Napthali continued, "brainwashing my black people, holding my black people in bondage, and teaching my black people to hate themselves. Well, once bitten twice shy — same dog bite you ah morning, he will bite you ah evening. "When Chris-teef Come-rob-us with all of his wicked intentions, my black African people saw our dreams an' aspirations crumble in front of our face. But if you know your history, then you will know where you're coming from. Then you wouldn't have to ask me, who the heck do I think I am. I an' I know seh we are African people. No matter where you come from, as long as you're a black man, you're an African. Even if your complexion is high, or it low, we are all Africans. Oh what a bumboclaat..."

Napthali suddenly perked up and rushed into his cave, returning moments later with a red, green and gold painted bongo drum on which he slapped a nyabinghi beat. The sound of the drumming echoed around the bay and, within moments, nearly every member of the encampment were joining in by banging a syncopated rhythm on their own drums. Johnny had to admit, they definitely had riddim.

"Follow me now," Napthali told Johnny, keeping the beat going. "Anyt'ing me seh, you say 'Proud to be black'... Marcus Garvey mek me..."

Almost mechanically, Johnny replied "Proud to be black."

"Bob Marley mek me..." Napthali chanted again.

"Proud to be black."

"Nelson Mandela mek me..."

"Proud to be black."

"Martin Luther King mek me..."

"Proud to be black."

"Malcolm X mek me…"

"Proud to be black."

"Harriet Tubman mek me…"

"Proud to be black."

"Winnie Mandela mek me…"

"Proud to be black."

"Muhammed Ali mek me…"

"Proud to be black."

Things were getting worse between Gussie and Linvall. When Gussie returned home late that night, he found that the door to their chalet in Las Vinas had been bolted from the inside. He banged on it hard and called out his friends' names. Nobody answered. Then he went around the other side to try the patio door. That too was locked. Gussie peered through the glass and his anger boiled inside him when he saw Linvall sitting on the living room couch watching television. Gussie banged on the door.

"Didn't you hear me calling?" he called out.

Whether Linvall could hear or not was immaterial, he wasn't answering.

Gussie's banging got louder.

"Linvall, don't let me have to break down this glass door. This is not funny any more. Just open up before I start getting ignorant."

Fortunately, Beres returned home at the same time from his dinner with Caroline and her boyfriend, and was able to let Gussie in before things got out of hand.

Gussie could barely restrain himself when he finally

got in. He was 'f-ing' and blinding and wanted to go for Linvall. But Beres stepped in between them. Linvall didn't even flinch a muscle.

"Just because you've got a minuscule willy, it's not my fault. You don't have to take it out on me."

That made Linvall explode. He jumped up and with all his might knocked Gussie backwards. The shove took Gussie by surprise, he lost his balance and fell back on his bottom with a hard thud due to all the weight he'd been putting on — the heavier they come, the harder they fall.

"Ever since we came to this bloody place, you've been taking the living liberties and acting like the don gorgon," Linvall warned him. "I ain't going to take it no more."

Beres was the man of reason, the man for all seasons. He managed to quieten his two friends down. After helping Gussie to his feet, he decided that they needed an emergency house meeting. He produced a bottle of rum from the kitchen and the three men sat down to iron out their differences.

Linvall told Gussie in no uncertain terms that he wasn't ever to bring up the size of his willy again. Neither was he to mention the name Emmanuelle or to spread rumours about his habits in bed. Gussie said that if Linvall hadn't lied in the first place about how big his willy used to be and about how he had performed excellently in bed with Emmanuelle, none of this would have happened in the first place. Most definitely.

Beres was just sitting back, not saying anything, but watching the ride as his friends threatened each other with grievous bodily harm. He thought the whole thing was incredibly childish and finally told them so. "Friends shouldn't be fighting over women," he said. Eventually, he managed to get Gussie and Linvall to shake hands and pretend kiss to make up.

"You know what this is all about, don't you?" Beres said. "We're all under manners because of our women. We came to Tene-grief to sort out one or two little problems, but it seems like we've spent our holiday dealing with new ones. I can't say it's funny having my wife here on the island with her new boyfriend. It's spoiled my entire holiday. But I'm trying to make the best of a good thing and if you two would give me a hand tomorrow night, I think I might just be able to save my marriage. Here's the plan…"

EL NUMERO UNO

The dawn began to suck the colour out of the sky. All that remained of the night was a paleness as the sun climbed the sky slowly, burning away the mist.

There is rhythm in the cool night air, like the beating heart of some massive animal. The drums of the white rasta encampment of Las Caletas had been pounding their hypnotic beat for six hours now and it didn't sound like they were going to be done for a good while yet. Long stretches of a simple nyabinghi beat punctuated by brief pauses. Then they would start up again with a fast drum roll.

The beat was almost spiritual, and had gotten inside Johnny's head and was stuck there. He felt like he'd been bouncing on his heels to the muffled beat for ever. The fact that he was experiencing a high like he had never experienced before didn't seem to help either. Johnny who thought that he was a connoisseur of good herb and had tasted the best there was, had now tasted one that could literally lick off his head. His entire environment seemed to be dancing around in slow motion. He couldn't seem to focus on where he was and who he was. He had lost his sense of touch. Jeez, this was more like tripping on acid or eating magic mushrooms than smoking a spliff.

Down below, in the deep black shadow of the raging ocean, he could just make out the wood fires of the other cave dwellers sparking their last embers into the night sky. The fires had earlier been sending up plumes of thick, choking smoke into the sky as they burned wood from the forest behind the bay, but they were now all but extinguished. The dogs that scrambled round their edges now lay in heaps around the ashes, supine, huddling for warmth, staring into the flames.

During the night the action was taking place all over the bay. Pipes were smoked around every camp fire, there had been enough marijuana to knock out an army. And to Johnny's embarrassment, the caucasians all seemed to be able to handle this crucial weed better than he!

The whole of the rasta encampment seemed to have come out of their caves for this impromptu rave dance. Adults and children alike were dancing outside their caves, arms outstretched as though welcoming the sun.

It must be really great to be brought up outside of conventional society, Johnny imagined as he watched the little kids dancing naked with no inhibitions. Still, he knew, one day these kids were going to be forced to conform. Whether they liked it or not.

"One good thing about music, when it hits you, you feel okay," Napthali said. He had been dancing non-stop for the last two hours and insisted that the dancing had rid him of all his stress. "You look tired, rasta. Here..." He passed Johnny the chalice once more. "Bu'n some weed, man, it will put some spirit back inna you."

Johnny declined, he had had enough spirit for one

night. He had better be getting back. He took a hurried leave of Napthali and started making his way back, the way he thought he had come.

Looking at the island on the map, anyone would think that the only way to make Tenerife feel bigger is to drive around it in huge circles. But Johnny could testify otherwise. He had been walking for four hours now and, although he felt that he must have circled the island a number of times, he hadn't arrived back at Playa de Las Americas. He had been walking through the dawn and into the early morning sunshine, along the coast, cutting across roads, down random lanes, through tiny villages, and along a straight hilltop lane fringed by fields of long grass, places tourists never bother to visit. He was lost. He was definitely lost. But he wasn't that bothered.

Still under the sensi, Johnny had been doing a lot of thinking throughout his walk. Whether it was the weed or whatever, Johnny started seeing his life so clearly. He came to the conclusion that he had played his cards wrong in life, he had gambled and lost. Nearly everybody he knew owned their own house, yet he wasn't even on the lowest rung of the housing market. He couldn't even afford the prices they were asking nowadays, if you hadn't worked your way onto the housing ladder already, you had to have a serious salary to afford even a cheap home. There were computer whizz kids of seventeen and eighteen earning much more than he was earning running The Book Shack in Peckham. He couldn't carry on living on a low wage. He was a big old man now, and he should at least have a mortgage. Those were the facts and reality.

It crossed his mind that going to Tanzania, as Beres had suggested, where they could accommodate his polygamous lifestyle, was an option. But it wasn't a realistic one. In the race of life he was lagging far behind the leaders and it wasn't clear whether or not he would make it, but he had made up his mind not to waste any more of his life. He was now going to do what he needed to do to get back on track and to realize that early potential he had had as a teenager. He had to change his foolish plans. He needed to rearrange his life and think positive. He needed to realize his abilities and succeed. He had to look at things from the 21st century black man point of view — money first. He knew he had enough lyrics in his mouth and cells in his brain to succeed at anything he put his mind to. All he had to do was apply himself. Application was what had been missing from his life since his school days. He'd lived the playa life for far too long and he didn't wanna be a playa no more. He didn't want to carry on living the way he used to. He didn't want two or three girls any more. All he needed was one woman who could turn his life around, a woman who wouldn't make him feel the need to go to other women, a woman who could satisfy his every need, a woman who he could live his whole life for...

Lesley would have been the ideal person, but if he went anywhere near her again, he was likely to get a jook in the eye, instead of where he would really like a jook. He needed a woman who could make a difference to his life, a woman who wouldn't just be there to take but was there to give him the things he needed also. Okay, his requirements for the ideal woman were high, but they were his requirements. If he found a woman who could fill them and she was interested, then they could work something out, but he wasn't going to make any more mistakes.

Easier said than done. Johnny knew that the problem of four kids by three different women was also on the agenda. He could find himself a new woman, but he couldn't walk away from his kids, he was umbilically tied to them for life whether he liked it or not. And they were his biggest burden, financially and otherwise. Oh, if he could only turn back the hands of time. If he could only start afresh from before he became a serial baby father, he would probably be a millionaire by now. But the reality was that he couldn't start afresh. He had made his bed and now he had to lie on it, his children's faces appeared vividly in his mind's eye to remind him.

Johnny hummed a haunting tune to the beat of his aching heart. He had come to a kind of clearing, on the edge of a field, which appeared to be a fallow field of grass and nettles. In the middle of the field was a flash of fluorescent lights. In one corner, what looked like a strobe flickered above the trees, like a giant discotheque in the sky. Johnny had to blink a couple of times. Were his eyes deceiving him? He made up his mind never to smoke a spliff again as long as he lived if this was the effect it was having on him. Then he made his way towards the beams of flickering light.

Thunder rumbled up in the heavens, and a bolt of lightning shot out of the sky. That was when the vision appeared. Dressed in shining armour upon a magnificent white steed, His Imperial Majesty, Emperor Haile Selassie I, King of Kings, Lord of Lords, Conquering Lion of the Tribe of Judah. Jah Rastafari appeared before Johnny.

Johnny was in a state of shock and automatically fell to the ground, his head bowed.

"If it's love that you're running from, there is no hiding place," the voice boomed from the sky. "But just put your faith in me, and you will leave all your troubles behind. And, remember, DO NOT COMMIT ADULTERY!"

With that, the vision was gone. Johnny had to rub his eyes again. Did he dream that? No, he was sure he didn't. It was the real thing. He had just had a visitation!

Not all the girls on the island were giving it up for free. There were lots of working girls there, too. Sometimes you couldn't even tell which was which. At least Gussie couldn't. The ladies on the streets of Playa de Las Americas at this time of night all looked like they were dressed in the same confusion.

His part in the plot was easy. All he had to do was procure the services of a lady of the night called Betty Boo.

Now Betty didn't come cheap at the best of times, but when she heard Gussie's proposal, she said that she always tripled her fee for pervs. Gussie tried to explain that he wasn't a perv. Betty said it was his word against hers. She had to trust her instincts. She had to protect herself. So it was triple or nothing.

Reluctantly, Beres paid up. After handing over the cash, he looked in his empty wallet. Betty had cleaned him out.

Linvall's role in the plot was even easier. All he had to do was stay undercover in Caroline's hotel lobby until she returned with Jean-Pierre from her evening out on the town. They didn't get back until two o'clock in the morning, by which time they were already merry. Linvall lifted a newspaper in front of his face as they walked past him. Then he waited for half an hour, before he went to one of the lobby phones and called Caroline's room.

Jean-Pierre picked up the phone.

"Zis is the hotel manager," Linvall said in his terrible spanish accent, "will Mrs Caroline Dunkley please come down to reception, zere seems to be a problem with her credit card."

"Can this not wait until morning?" Jean-Pierre snapped.

"No, I am afraid not. I have to request that she comes down immediately otherwise I will be left with no choice but to call the police."

"Okay, I'll come down and sort it out," Jean-Pierre said.

"No, I am afraid not, sir, Mrs Dunkley has to come down in person."

A moment later, Caroline came on the line. Linvall explained that the credit card company had reported as stolen the credit card she was using to pay her hotel bills.

Caroline huffed and puffed, but under the threat of the police being called, she thought that she had better go down and sort out this storm in a teacup. She threw on a baggy jumper and a pair of slacks and made her way down to reception none too amused.

Beres had gambled on Jean-Pierre staying up in their room on the eighth floor. He was waiting on the floor below, and when the lift descended with Caroline in it, it stopped on the seventh floor. Caroline was so frustrated at being called down to reception in the middle of the night that she didn't even notice the man who had stepped into the lift, although she could smell the distinct aroma of alcohol following him in. The doors closed and the lift descended again. He stood behind her for a few seconds, observing the back of her head. Then, suddenly, the lift came to an abrupt stop.

"Damn!" Caroline said, pushing the button for the ground floor repeatedly.

Beres took another swig of the bottle of cider in his hand.

"Caroline, is that you?" he slurred drunkenly.

"Oh!" Caroline was startled. In her tiredness she had almost forgotten that there was someone else in the lift. "Beres! What are you doing here?" She was immediately suspicious.

"I just came by to visit a friend who's staying at this hotel," he said. He giggled a drunken giggle and slurred his words some more. "We've been-*hic*-drinking, it was very naysh-*hic*!"

Caroline was still not convinced, she was a barrister after all. Something smelt fishy to her, not just the alcohol. But she had only circumstantial evidence which would not stand up in court. Anyway, it was more important to get out of this lift.

"What a coincidence," Beres smiled. "*Hic!*'

Caroline told him that she hadn't forgotten nor forgiven him for the other night when he slipped out of the restaurant without paying and for wasting her time. So, if he wouldn't mind keeping his mouth shut while she tried to get them out of this...

She pressed the alarm. Nothing. She pressed again, still nothing. She started banging on the door and shouting. But only Beres heard her cries and he seemed too drunk to care.

Beres could see how tired and frustrated Caroline was.

"There's nothing much we can do for the moment," he said, "but *sh*omeone's bound to come a-*hic*-long soon enough."

Meanwhile, he decided there was nothing to do but make polite conversation with his estranged wife.

"You know what I've learned in the last few weeks-*hic*," he began, "is that love, REAL love, is never having to *sh*ay you're *sh*orry — even if you have accidentally torn up your woman's new *sh*ilk-*hic*-blouse and you've been using it to-*hic*-polish your car. Like the *sh*ong *sh*ays, 'all you need is love and everything can be forgiven'."

Caroline snapped back that she didn't remember the

song going like that.

"Look, I don't want to be a repressing macho pig, invading your *sh*pace and continuing the historical *sh*exism of my gender group," Beres countered, "but can we continue this conver*sh*ation in horizontal mode?"

Caroline would have slapped him there and then, but she was a lawyer and knew all about people going to jail for assault.

"Look, I know how you feel, Caroline, but we've got much more going for us than to let one indiscretion ruin it all. I refuse to regret the past. My philosophy on life is that, you are what your life has made you and to regret past experiences would be to regret one's whole life. It's happened, it's happened. What I have to do now, is try to become a better father to my daughter and, perhaps one day, I'll make a better husband to you. I will never give up hope. Look, I don't rate myself as very romantic, but I reckon I know what turns you on. You like a man with charm, intelligence, personality factors, good figure, face, humour, wit, good legs, beautiful eyes, a nice tight bottom, who dresses well and has good hair and kissable lips. So what are you doing with Jean-Pierre, when you could have me?"

Caroline smirked. If Beres really knew what she wanted, he would never have been unfaithful.

"Oh, but I do know you. I know that you don't want a strongwilled man, but at the same time you don't want a sensitive man (which is just as well, since I don't consider myself sensitive). I know you want passion, sensuality and tenderness and understanding. A man who senses your requirements. I also know that you want your man to be well-endowed, though you're the least likely to say that size is important. I know you want your man's performance in bed to be a lot better than average and that you like to give as well as receive pleasure."

"If you're trying to tell me that Jean-Pierre is my perfect man, I already know that. I don't need you telling me. It's none of your business." She was unmoved and looked passively as him. "So you're not drunk any more?" she asked.

Beres wasn't drunk at all. He had had one 'depth charger' (a little bit of spirit in a glass of cider) and he had poured some cider over his clothes. He needed Caroline to take him back to her hotel room with her. He wanted to be there when she discovered that all men were alike, that Jean-Pierre was no different from him.

But Caroline was no fool. She knew Beres better than he knew himself. In the year that they had been married, she had never once seen him drunk. In fact, she had seen him polish off a bottle of rum, followed by a bottle of whisky and still be able to keep it up all night long as they made passionate love. There was definitely something fishy going on. She pushed all the buttons on the lift and banged on the doors some more.

"Apart from my one indiscretion," Beres continued, reverting back to slurring his words, "you cant shay I didn't treat you with love and respect."

"What are you trying to say?" she asked unbelievingly at the stupidity. "Are you trying to say being unfaithful only once is still loving and respectful?"

"Being angry with me for making things bad won't help," Beres reasoned.

"It isn't anger, anyway, or pride, or anything like that. I'm not proud. I was hurt though."

"I understand, and the only way you can deal with hurt is through comfort. I'm here to comfort you," Beres put a reassuring arm around her.

If Beres felt that Caroline should give him a break and that she should accept that he was really the right man for her, and that when you looked at it from his point of view he hadn't done much wrong, Caroline felt the complete opposite.

She shrugged his arm off her and spelt it out for him.

"You left the good life you had for fuss and fight and now you want to come back into my life..."

She didn't get much further than that because the lift suddenly jerked into movement. Upwards. Back to the eighth floor. Caroline stormed out of the lift and made her way back to her room. She would call the manager in reception and vent her displeasure at being stuck in a lift with a drunken man for ten minutes. If the manager wanted to sort this credit card problem out, he would have to come up to her.

She had barely slotted her keycard in the door than Beres barged in behind her, holding his mouth as if he was going to vomit.

"Sorry, I've got to use your bathroom... I'm about to throw up..."

Moments after Caroline had left her room to go down to

reception, there was a knock on her hotel room door. Jean-Pierre had jumped up to open it, expecting to find Caroline had returned to collect something she'd forgotten. To his surprise, Betty Boo pushed her way in.

"Quick, we don't have much time," Betty had said hurriedly.

Jean-Pierre was perplexed.

"Who are you?" he said.

"Room service with a smile," Betty said, opening her overcoat for him to see that she had nothing to hide except for stockings and suspenders.

Jean-Pierre almost collapsed. "Get out! Get out!!" He screamed, aware that Caroline could return at any moment.

But Betty Boo was an expert at her job. She had already grabbed Jean-Pierre by the balls and unzipped his trousers. By now Jean-Pierre's cock was standing to attention, despite himself. But he couldn't speak. This woman had him literally by the balls and, as any man knows, it felt soooooooooooooo good. As Betty worked her mouth on him, he couldn't help sighing with satisfaction, even though he should have been screaming. Okay, he was thinking to himself, work your stuff, but make it quick. It sure is niiiiiiiiiiiiiiiiiiiice!

And Betty Boo did make it quick. Jean-Pierre came within seconds. That was the first time. The second time took a little longer, about a minute. The third time no more than ninety seconds.

By the time Beres, followed by Caroline, burst into the room, Jean-Pierre had come six times and Betty Boo was working on the seventh.

Baby Father 3: *Does my batty look big in this?*

Caroline stood there in shock. Even Beres, who had set up the whole thing couldn't believe how well it had gone. All Caroline could say was, "Who is this woman?"

But Betty wasn't a woman. Sure, she had breasts, but she also had a ginormous penis which was, possibly, even bigger than Beres'.

Patrick Augustus

EPILOGUE

Ladies, they say some guys have all the luck, well, a year ago, Jonathan Lindo was just another south London ragamuffin juggling to make ends meet. 365 days later, he has become the most eligible black bachelor in Britain. Not only is he the sole owner of a multimillion pound business empire, he's also recently been declared 'The Best Dressed Man in Britain', and he's not bad in the looks department either.

To say that Jonathan Lindo's rise to success was phenomenal is an understatement. This tall, cool, dark-brown complexioned, clean-shaven, good-looking unassuming twentysomething is one of Britain's fresh crop of sharp entrepreneurs, having shaken up the business community with the astonishingly dramatic rise in his fortunes. His business alone is now worth £21 million! Add to that the £4.2 million he won on the National Lottery recently and you'll figure out why he became the second black man to make it into the Sunday Times 'Rich List'. He's now the proud owner of a Porsche Turbo, a Mercedes convertible, two Lexuses and a Jaguar XJS saloon with personal plates - JON $$$.

His is a story of a young brotha's virtual rise from rags to riches. Now he has gained not only the admiration of young hustlers-to-be, but also the respect of some of the country's top business people.

Despite all this good fortune, it is a surprise to discover that Jonathan Lindo is still a bachelor and that he can't seem to find a woman.

He has a smile to die for (Oh, that smile!) and a deep dimple on his left cheek (Only one dimple!) Sitting in his mock tudor Surrey mansion set in three acres of landscaped gardens, one is immediately struck by Jonathan's restless ambition and his air of easy confidence.

But his outward persona belies a personal grief, a wound beneath the skin which has never properly healed, and which, in a sense, has come to define him.

He told me why he is still a lonely lover.

"I've worked hard over the last year trying to make a success of my business. I've worked seven days a week, sixteen hours a day. I'm afraid I haven't made much time for 'affairs of the heart'. Regretfully. Now, I've got all the money in the world but, believe me, money can't buy love. I'm living proof of that. But I've been rich and I've been poor and, trust me, rich is better.

"I used to believe that a man must always stay in control of things. And my idea of staying in control was to take care of business first and enjoy myself with a woman second. But now I realize that I have had my priorities wrong all the time. If there was just one woman out there, who I could settle down and live with, I'd make her my wife and she'd be entitled to half of everything I have. I'm living alone now and looking for the next relationship, which I hope will be the last one."

Ladies, before you all rush out to send this dishy, well-spoken young millionaire a photograph of yourselves, he's not just looking for any and everybody. Jonathan gave me a list of his requirements for his dream lady:

Patrick Augustus

She has to have the class and poise to go with his millionaire jetsetting lifestyle and not be phased by meeting some of the top black American celebrities who regularly stop by his penthouse suite overlooking the Thames in Vauxhall.

She has to be able to look beautiful and glamorous at all times, whether she's accompanying him to a garden party at Buckingham Palace or whether she's just sunbathing on the deck of his yacht The Reggae Boy *currently moored in St. Tropez in the south of France.*

She has to have a university education. Please no dibby-dibby girls need apply.

She has to have ambition.

She has to have the confidence to deal with a relationship in which her partner is much more successful than she is, without feeling inferior.

She has to be able to cook homestyle Caribbean dishes.

And she must want to bear at least three children.

"I know other single men who are still waiting for Miss Right. But what's the point. I don't think she exists. Better to find someone who will suffice and just get on with it. But if any woman out there can fulfill all my requirements, I would like to hear from her," Johnny continued.

"Some may think that I am just a lucky chap to have

achieved such vast wealth in only a year, but it's got nothing to do with luck. Even my lottery win is more about destiny than luck. You see, what the past year has taught me is that nothing in life is impossible to accomplish. You make it if you try. People never believed I could reach the top. They even put stumbling blocks in my way, but my ambition was stronger than their desire to see me fail. I made it through. Now all those who hated me are patting me on my back to congratulate me, and they all want to be my friends.

"Ambition is the key to holding your own future in your hand. Ambition is the key to any door. Read my new book, As Rich As You Wanna Be *and follow all the instructions. Read a page a day and you'll see how your wisdom increases. Because, let's face it, rich is what we all want to be and the opportunity is there, if you're willing to work seven days a weeks and if you're prepared to unlock every door to success."*

It was the first interview that Johnny had ever granted. Okay, he lobbed a decade off his age, but apart from that he had been relatively modest, considering. Since he made his first million, there had been several requests for interviews from, particularly though not exclusively, the black press. But he had always declined, saying that in the course of a ten minute interview he could have done a deal worth £40,000 to him and, unless the paper were prepared to reimburse him for that loss, he couldn't really afford to give one. But this interview was different. The editor herself had been on his case. She had wooed him and wined and dined him at every opportunity, and used all her feminine charms on him. And she had plenty of those.

She had taken him to her favourite brasserie at the Savoy Hotel, overlooking the Thames. They were, of course, the only black people in the place, the other guests being the rich and famous from Britain and abroad — air-kissing fashion, PR, media and music industry types. Between courses of poached salmon and lobster, washed down with the most expensive champagne, Jenny Stewart turned on all her womanly charms to get this most elusive of bachelors to open up to her. If not for the article...

Johnny wasn't surprised at Jenny's initial question. It was the first thing on most people's mind.

"So what's it like being rich?" she had asked.

"Better than being poor," he replied, and then he smiled as if only for her.

It was a standard reply which he had practiced and executed a thousand times in the last year.

It didn't take long for Jenny to get on to the subject that she was really interested in.

"So how come a black man like you, with everything going for him, is still single?"

Johnny smiled as she asked the question that he knew would eventually be asked. He had prepared a suitable reply with lots of 'sound bites'. His mind couldn't help but conjure up images of the many other women who had asked the same question in the past year. He thought of all the responses he had used in the past, only to find that the answer always came down to the same thing, he simply was not ready. And that's what he told Jenny.

But things are never that simple with a story-hungry

journalist. For no sooner had Johnny given the explanation than Jenny started probing as if he had something to hide.

"What do you mean, you aren't ready? It's not like you're not old enough to get married."

Johnny smiled again. Jenny obviously didn't realize that it was the same point that he wrestled himself with on a daily basis. Now that he had all this wealth, he wanted someone to share it all with. But he didn't want just any old person. He certainly didn't want to be tied to the wrong woman 'til death do us part'.

"Marriage is disappointing for a lot of black men because, for so many, even if they work hard on making it happen, it doesn't. And then it becomes a shattered dream. I've known so many black men with shattered dreams that I decided a long time ago that I wouldn't be one of them. I decided then that when I take the plunge it will be for ever. In which case, I've got to find the right woman. But it's all good, you can still have good experiences if you're single."

Jenny's journalistic instincts were homing in. This was too good to be true. If Jonathan Lindo was for real, this would be the interview of the year, she would become journalist of the year. She might even win a Pulitzer... The sound of Johnny's deep voice brought her back to earth.

"I don't even have time for dating these days. I'm keeping busy making power moves. But as busy as I am," he continued, "I admit that I would gladly make room for a wife and family. But I believe that marrying or having children grows less likely with each passing

day. I really believe I will probably never get married,"
he said, adding that sometimes it made him feel sad.

A tear almost came to Jenny's eye as Johnny spoke.
She couldn't believe that she was getting sentimental
over this guy. Where was her journalistic cynicism?
Where was her hard editor (tough as nails) armour that
she always wore when meeting with movers and
shakers? Was she losing it? Or was Jonathan Lindo just
too good to be real?

"When I was younger, I thought that life would turn
out differently. Back then I thought I would be married
by the time I was twenty-one. But things didn't work
out. Sometimes I consider adopting a child, because
when I peer into the future it can seem lonesome. I think
about growing old by myself. Someone asked me the
other day whether I regretted not being married. I said
no, I didn't. But I'm not so sure now."

"What about kids, I bet you've got loads of baby
mothers all over the place. I don't know a single black
man of your age who doesn't have a kid somewhere or
other," Jenny prodded.

"Well, you're looking at one now. I think you'll find
that there isn't a child on this earth who knows me as
daddy. Some of us black men are responsible, you know.
Sure, I've had many opportunities to take the baby
father route in life if I wanted to, goodness knows I've
known several women who would have obliged, but
I'm a different breed of black man. I'm a modern day
black man, and we think very deeply before we go and
make a mistake like that. Besides, I would never have
made a success of my business if I had had obligations

towards any offspring. So many of my friends became fathers after school and then gave up on the careers they were aiming for. I feel privileged to say that didn't happen to me."

Jenny was ecstatic. This would make a fantastic story. She could see the headlines now: New Black Man Speaks Out/ The Lonely/Millionaire/ From Ragga To Riches... She knew that she had to get Jonathan to agree to let her get all this down on tape and to let her publish it in her magazine. Whatever it took, she wanted to be the first person to penetrate the 'no-interview' exterior of Jonathan Lindo III, the fastest rising black businessman in Britain. His story couldn't have been better if she had made it up herself: He went to church most Sundays and had the Midas touch in business during the week. He is still single, but thinks about marriage, though a more compelling goal in life, he says, is to be at peace with himself. The nationals would lap up this story. The thought of seeing her byline in *The Sunday Times* magazine and possibly even in *Time* and *Newsweek*, gave Jenny a mini orgasm and; despite herself, she let out a soft sigh of pleasure.

The next twenty minutes or so were taken up with Johnny explaining to Jenny that his hesitation with marriage was simply an attempt to keep his head focused.

"I've learned from past experience that when a man takes a woman into his life, he must be prepared to dedicate his life to her spiritual, physical and mental well-being. A man's life thus takes on an almost contrived, artificial dimension because of all the

211

expectations that he will have to deliver. All of a sudden you have to become a 'husband', committed until the day you die. And though these are all things I seek in a relationship, I prefer to stay well away from temptation until I have found the woman I am prepared to dedicate my life and soul to."

"But what about sex? I bet you don't say no to a grind when it's put before you on a platter," Jenny challenged mischievously.

Johnny didn't dignify that question with an answer. The conversation was getting a little too personal now and he felt like asking Jenny to please butt out of his business. Jenny's desire to play psychiatrist was, however, already heightened and she now found it necessary to be made aware of every little habit, peculiarity or shortcoming that Johnny might possess.

"What is it you're trying to hide, Jonathan? Or what is it about you that you don't want me to discover?"

"I'm not trying to hide anything," Johnny protested.

"Then, answer the question. What about sex? Are you able to resist that as you are able to resist marriage?"

Johnny wasn't blind. He could see in Jenny's eyes where this was leading to. He could see that she wanted to him to put an arm around her and give her a squeeze. He wasn't stupid either. He knew that she would like nothing better than for him to say 'I'm crazy 'bout you, let's go to bed' or, better still, 'Let's get married'. It was a funny thing this millionaire's life. Because wealth means power and, in Johnny's experience, there was nothing that turned women on like a man with power.

He had so much power, he could make men bow down and lick his shoes. Even police officers treated him with respect. Everywhere he went there was a string of people ready to kiss his arse at the first request to do so. And there was an infinite number of women who wouldn't mind going to bed with him just to get a chance of sleeping with power. If this was a year previously, he would have taken full advantage of the situation. But, then again, he didn't have the wealth nor the power a year ago.

Johnny moved his knee until it brushed Jenny's soft thigh under the table. She didn't push his knee away.

No, as tempting as it was to reach under the table with one hand and spread Jenny's legs wide apart whilst his other hand searched for the treasures that lay between them, his days of taking risks with his life, career and fortune in order to have sex with a desired woman were over.

In truth, he had been without a woman for a year, despite the many propositions, as his wheel of fortune spun round and round. Enduring a stretch of celibacy was a small price to pay for all the material riches the world had to offer. He told Jenny as much, and that he couldn't ever envisage a time when a woman would be able to tempt him in that way again.

Jenny took that as a challenge.

"I bet I could make you lose your mind enough to be tempted."

"I bet you can't," Johnny replied confidently.

She took the bet on. If she won he would grant her that exclusive interview she was after. If he won… Well, she had nothing to offer except that she would leave him alone and not pester him for a formal interview.

Johnny had no doubt in his mind that he was 'untemptable'. It would be worth the exercise just to prove to himself that even a sizzling hot woman like Jenny Stewart couldn't get him to ignore his principles.

They had had a particularly good time together. Johnny insisted on picking up the bill and said that he looked forward to "doing lunch again, sometime."

"How about tomorrow?" Jenny offered.

She didn't give Johnny a chance to refuse. She managed to get him to part with his home address and promised that she would be there the next day to win her bet.

"Or lose it, as the case may be," Johnny smiled.

"We'll see," Jenny said mysteriously.

Maybe it was Fate which boomed down on him, but it was a mystery to Johnny how Jenny figured out that his one remaining unfulfilled sexual fantasy was a four-in-a-bed romp. Perhaps it was just a coincidence, but the next afternoon three dark beauties by the names of Eenie-Meenie, Miney and Mo arrived at Jenny's appointed time at the door of Johnny's millionaire mansion in an exclusive road in Purley. He froze, muscles rigid when he opened the door to them, for they were practically shoving their breasts in his face.

"Hi," said Eenie-Meenie, the tallest of the three, thrusting herchest forward so that her breasts were practically in his mouth. With a cheeky smile, she tweaked the crutch of his jeans and felt his manhood rise.

"We've come to fulfill your every fantasy."

Johnny's heart jumped at the words. His eyes travelled over her sleek waist, focused at last on her wide womanly hips. Even the sound of her purring voice, feminine and sexy, stirred him. Remember, this was a man who had been celibate for over a year.

What Eenie-Meenie, Miney and Mo lacked in savoir-faire, they certainly made up for in dimples and batting eyelashes. Johnny breathed deeply, then ushered the three women inside.

The ladies didn't waste any time. Mo, whose platinum blonde wig juxtaposed strikingly against her dark chocolate skin, had summoned her sweetest expression as her small fingers began unbuttoning Johnny's sports shirt. Johnny liked her smile and the stylish clothes she wore — a gorgeous black silk and sequinned dress with matching new shoes, the kind with spiked heels so high your nose bleeds.

Miney's hand had already worked its way down the front of Johnny's trousers, and she led him by the cock up the stairs to the no-expenses-spared master bedroom, with ensuite bathroom.

"What I do best is suck men off," she said seductively.

Her lips suggested a hint of pink lipstick, while her eyes promised that she was going to give Johnny the best blow job he had ever had and that was an experience that no man in their right mind would turn down.

Meanwhile, Eenie-Meenie had unbuttoned her blouse to reveal that she wasn't a 'meanie' at all, but was willing to share all of her generously-sized breasts with Johnny. She shoved one in his face and nearly smothered him.

The escort agency business offers every conceivable kind of service. The agency Jenny Stewart had hired, had as its motto: 'Your desire is our pleasure...' They charged £150 per hour, per model, but Jenny wasn't perturbed about it. For one thing, everything was being charged to the magazine, and though the total bill (with VAT) would be well over a grand, it was money well worth spending to be able to secure a scoop such as an exclusive first interview with Jonathan Lindo III.

Besides, Eenie-Meenie, Miney and Mo were very professional at their job. They didn't need to ask the customer's name. That was considered impolite in the trade, and anyway it made no difference. The customer was king (or queen, as the case may be) and their job was to fulfill his/her wishes.

The escort game was such a good earner, that for Eenie-Meenie, Miney and Mo, it wasn't so much a hobby, as a career, and they took pride in doing their job as well as possible. By now, Eenie-Meenie had her skirt unzipped, and her slender fingers rolled down her silk panties.

Lying with his back on the kingsize divan in the master bedroom, Johnny closed his eyes and remained perfectly still while the three escorts stripped him naked and went to work caressing and kissing every single part of his body.

Baby Father 3: *Does my batty look big in this?*

Like a striking yellow cobra, Miney uncoiled from the bed and hooked her arms around Johnny's waist, and sank her teeth into his cock. Johnny moaned with a mixture of pleasure and pain as Miney worked on it slowly.

"Aaaaaaaaaaaaaaggggggggggh!" Johnny gasped. She was certainly an expert in the art.

In just one year, all Johnny's dreams had been realized. He had become one of the richest guys out there and, moreover, had realized his one remaining sexual fantasy. It seemed like he had everything a man could possible ask for.

Mo, meanwhile, had hitched up her dress and sat on his face, giving Johnny a mouthful of muff. The punnany was too sweet to resist.

With her legs astride him on the bed, Eenie-Meenie purred invitingly, "Come on, big poppa come and get some sugar-honey-iced-tea."

Johnny couldn't wait. His cock stood to attention. Peering down her back, seeing the seductive rise of her full rear, he smiled to himself. This was to be savoured. Her fingers rested on her hips, massaging slightly. He was hungry for a woman. Any woman. It had been 428 days since he last enjoyed the pleasures of intercourse. He slipped his hand between her soft thighs and rubbed her clitoris, his finger as light as a feather. He savoured every second as Eenie-Meenie orbited above him and then descended slowly until he had entered her.

"It's soooooooooo beautiful!" he gasped.

Eenie-Meenie had been in the business long enough to say the very things a client wanted to hear. *"You* are so beautiful." she replied.

She rocked him gently. He moaned, eyes closed.

"Oh, baby, faster. Faster," he urged.

Meanwhile, Miney had begun to work on his ringpiece with a huge dildo, still in its wrapper marked *African Black Magic xtra large*, which she produced seemingly out of thin air.

"I-I-I... It's soooooooo beautiful." Johnny cried tears of joy. He turned and kissed Mo, and gently spread her legs.

"Shhhhhhh!" Mo said, putting a finger to her lips. There was no need for words. "It will be beautiful, special, I promise."

By the time each woman had done her job, Johnny was exhausted but not too exhausted to start again. He was enjoying it so much, in fact, that he hadn't even noticed that the time had been slipping and sliding by and that the ladies had been there for three hours already. It was now time to bring proceedings to a reluctant end.

"Maybe we could go on a date some time," Johnny suggested as the ladies stepped into the shower together to freshen up.

"We never mix business with pleasure," Eenie-Meenie retorted.

Spiritually and otherwise, Johnny was never the same after his experiences in Tenerife. He didn't return to Britain with his friends after their week's holiday on the island, but had spent forty days and forty nights meditating up in the hills overlooking Playa de las Americas. Fortunately, he had one of his miniature Gideon Bibles with him and he went through its contents like never before. Suddenly, he wasn't just reading verses written two thousand years ago. Now those verses had real meaning. The Bible wasn't just something you picked up and read on a Sunday, it was the key to life, Johnny now realized. Hidden within its pages was the answer to that nagging question every human being has to face at some point: What is the correct way to live your life?

The first thing that Johnny did when he returned to England was look in his bank account. There was just eighty-six pence inside. He promised himself that he wasn't going to live like that again.

With the holiday money he had left, he was able to pay a month's deposit on a tiny bedsit in Hackney, north London, which he decorated with a plaque that he had picked up at an army surplus store earlier. It had the inscription 'who dares wins'.

It was the first time that Johnny had ever lived north of the river, the first time he had ever lived in a neighbourhood where he didn't know most of the playas in the area, which was just as well as he needed to keep a low profile while he fulfilled the prophecy. With the little money he had left, he was just about able to scrape together enough to buy a cheap suit and a pair of black brogues. Dressed very professionally, he managed to get a job at an estate agents with no trouble. He needed to make some quick cash.

Johnny started getting up at the crack of dawn and

running five miles on Hackney Downs every morning
to stay in shape. Then he would work like there was no
tomorrow. Sixteen hours a day if he had to. Hell, if it
meant closing on a deal, he would work around the
clock if necessary. This was probably going to be the last
chance he would have in life to achieve his destiny of
being successful. In a few years time he would be too
old to work this hard.

He saved every penny he could. He didn't go out,
but stayed at home every evening reading all the
business books he could borrow from the local library.
Staying at home studying how to make money was
more important than raving, he decided. By day he
showed clients around houses in Stoke Newington.

For every day that went by, yet another trace of the
old Johnny Dollar was being erased. Johnny no longer
spoke with the mixture of English cockney and patois
that he had cultivated over the years, but now reverted
to the polished, correct pronunciation that he had
learned in his school days. He had also stopped
smoking herb, for no other reason than that he couldn't
afford it. He needed every penny he could save. With
regard to his dreadlocks, Johnny could not bring
himself to accept that they were gone. It was a subject
that he did not which to comment on, but he now
sported a neat, low fade.

It didn't take him long to learn the tricks of the
business. Selling houses was like child's play. All you
had to do was sweet talk your clients into imagining
that this was the home of their dreams, and good value
at that. Johnny always made out that he had shown

several other people the property and that they seemed
keen too, and that this was a once in a lifetime
opportunity. What he didn't tell his clients, was that he
stood to earn a good commission for every contract
exchanged.

He had sold a total of nine properties in the first
three months of working there. It was then that he
found his first property. It was a five-storey Victorian
house on Amhurst Road, in which an old lady had lived
by herself since she was widowed twenty years before.
Now in her nineties, her children were keen to push her
into a nursing home so that they could share the profits
from the sale of the house amongst themselves. They
wanted a quick sale and were prepared to take less than
the market value.

Johnny saw his opportunity and arranged a fast track
mortgage for himself with some contacts he had
nurtured during his three months at the estate agents. It
meant having to juggle a few figures or, in truth, having
to inflate his salary by five hundred percent and telling
an untruth or two about how long he had been working
there, but it was surprisingly easy to borrow the sum he
required.

Within two weeks he had exchanged contracts. Two
weeks on from that, he had sold the house again for a
tidy profit, all of which went on the purchase of his next
house.

It didn't take long for Johnny to get the house buying
bug. He surprised himself about how much he had
learned about the housing market in the few short
months he had been working at the estate agents. He

allowed himself to be guided by his golden rule number one: What makes an area desirable is that there is a queue of people who want to live there. What makes a house desirable is that it's in the right area and it's as good a home, or better, than any other in the vicinity.

Six months later, Johnny had bought and sold a dozen houses in different parts of London and was now buying and selling at the rate of three or four houses a month. The stakes were getting higher and higher as he bought ever more expensive properties.

It was then that Johnny made his first millions.

The local council had sold him a row of properties in the Hoxton Square area which had remained derelict for many years. In fact, when Johnny first went to visit them, they had been inhabited by a flock of pigeons who were rather reluctant to be evicted from their homes of many years.

The decision to sell these properties cheap to a property speculator who had plans to turn them into an exclusive residential complex of loft style apartments for upwardly mobile city types, was leaked anonymously to the local press and caused an uproar within the left wing local council which was having problems trying to house its many homeless constituents. It was such an unpopular political decision, that the council leader was forced to overturn the decision of his housing officer and demanded that the properties should be bought back immediately. Johnny had no problem with that, only now he intended to sell the properties back at the market rate, which was several times what he had agreed to buy them for.

Baby Father 3: *Does my batty look big in this?*

Some guys have all the luck. As if this unexpected windfall wasn't enough, Johnny also became a jackpot winner of the National Lottery that weekend, which added several millions more to his fortune.

The first Linvall knew of Johnny's cup overflowing with good fortune was when Marcia handed him the article she had just finished reading in *Headwraps* magazine. He hadn't seen his friend since Johnny disappeared in Tenerife. None of them had. He hadn't phoned, he hadn't written or contacted anybody at all in more than a year. It was las if Johnny had fallen off the face of the earth. But, no, here he was larger than life and a multi-millionaire to boot. Linvall couldn't believe it. He could barely recognize his friend without his dreadlocks.

It didn't take Linvall long to get in touch with Johnny through the magazine.

Johnny was delighted to see his old friend again. They embraced like long lost friends when Linvall arrived at Johnny's mansion in Purley.

"Boy, you're living large!" Linvall complimented his friend. He certainly approved of the furnishings and fittings of the millionaire home and approved even more when Johnny pressed a buzzer on his desk to summon the butler to bring some refreshments.

"So what have you been up to, old boy," said Johnny, slapping Linvall on the back cheerfully.

Linvall filled him in on all that had been happening since they last met in Tenerife.

"Gussie's now a baby father. He got a letter from the

CSA demanding payments for the twins the other day. He's not too happy about it, as you can imagine. He's drinking heavily and getting fatter. He says he doesn't give a fuck. Beres is back together with Caroline, but I don't see much of him because he's too busy being a househusband. Caroline was only prepared to take him back on those terms. I'm the same as ever. Same old same old. Still trying to be there for my son, Lacquan. He's a bit more strong-willed than he used to be. But we are very good friends. It's me and him against the world and we seem to be winning. But enough about me. What about you? What happened to you, man. Haven't seen you in over a year. We searched all over Tenerife for you, but couldn't find you."

Johnny gave Linvall a brief summary of the last 365 days.

"…I began to re-evaluate my life, and I could see that it was an appalling misery. It was miserable… I rented a room, on the first night a rat ran across my chest… But the thing I remember most is the immense feeling of relief."

"So what happened to your locks, man?"

Johnny recalled that day in the barber saloon. Even the barber couldn't believe that a rastaman was prepared to trim his locks so readily. He informed Johnny of how many other barbers had gone bust due to the rise in locks men in the area.

"What about Selassie I? What about Samson and Delilah?" the barber teased him as he shaved Johnny's head. "Don't you know that Jah ah go strike you dead if you ah turn baldhead?"

By now a large crowd had gathered outside the barber shop to watch this dreadlocks get shorn, it was the first time any of them had witnessed such a sight. A few enterprising young schoolboys were selling Wrigleys, oranges and roasted peanuts to the gathered throng. One or two rastamen amongst the crowd shouted through the barber's pane glass window, hurling curses on Johnny's head.

"Fire bu'n 'pon you!"

"You can't nevah go to Zion now!"

Johnny didn't want to talk about it, but in his heart felt that his locks were a small price to pay for all the riches of the world.

They sat and chatted for several hours. Linvall could not quite come to terms with how the Johnny Dollar he had known so well for so long had changed quite so much. It wasn't just the locks, it was the posh accent, the mannerisms, and everything else. Linvall had mixed feelings about Johnny's great transformation and secretly wished the old Johnny came back. But he didn't say so.

"Since that article in *Headwraps* magazine, the whole of Brixton knows that you're blowing up like nitro. All those guys you used to roll dice with, smoke spliff with and get nice with are looking a non-refundable loan off you. They heard about the Rolexes and the Lexuses. They heard about your your mansion and the seaside home in Jamaica that you bought your mum, and they feel that you must have a spare hundred grand lying around that you don't need."

Johnny laughed. He wasn't surprised. Another

225

funny thing about wealth, the moment you have it people start popping out of the woodwork to remind you about how they always supported you from back in the day and asking whether you could find it in your heart to pay back some of that support with a few grand.

"So, how are all your baby mothers taking this new found wealth of yours? I'm surprised that they're not here now distressing you for some."

"What baby mothers?" Johnny replied with a confused look on his face.

"You know, Lesley, Pauline and that other one you got pregnant the other day."

"What are you talking about..."

Selective amnesia is a funny thing. Johnny had no recollection of the fact that he had children by any woman. Linvall thought Johnny was having him on. He tried for the next three hours to jog Johnny's memory, but his friend didn't give the slightest hint that he knew what Linvall was going on about.

"Well, you might have forgotten them, but they definitely won't have forgotten you. Not now that you've got all this loot."

With those parting words, Linvall departed, promising to hook up again at the weekend.

Linvall's words would prove to be prophetic.

So much for oaths of celibacy, once that article appeared, Johnny was inundated with offers from willing women from all over the world (six mailsacks full) who were ready and waiting to be his Cinderella, if he would just say the word and become their prince. He also received twenty sackfulls of begging letters from people saying that they hadn't eaten for six days and if he could find it in his heart to send them a cheque for £20,000 or so, the Lord would bless him. Several of those letters also quoted a line from the Bible about it being easier for a camel to pass through the eye of a needle than for a rich man to be welcomed into the kingdom of heaven.

The next few weeks were just one long dating session for Johnny. Amongst the women who had sent him their photographs, he selected a couple of hundred who he felt were worth checking.

It was a punishing schedule, but Johnny was determined that every one of these women would get a chance to be his wife. A typical day would start with him meeting up with Miss A for lunch followed by a couple of hours of rumpy pumpy. By five o'clock, having disposed of a well satisfied Miss A, he would go and collect Miss B for cocktails at his mansion which would usually conclude with the bedsprings in the master bedroom marking time as Miss B tried to convince him that she should marry him because she had the 'wickedest slam'. He would arrange to meet Miss C in the West End in time to catch a nine-thirty movie. Miss C was usually dispatched home with passionate kisses and 'oohs' and 'aahs' by midnight, at which point Johnny would rush back to his penthouse in Vauxhall by twelve-fifteen to the voluptuous Miss D who would invariably spend the night or most of it with him. It helped sometimes that Miss D was mobile and could therefore leave graciously before daylight, when Miss E. would arrive.

Jenny Stewart sent Johnny a copy of the next month's issue of *Headwraps*, with a note from her suggesting that he should check out the letters page.

The 'Letter of the Month' was a bitter attack on Johnny.

Dear Headwraps,

I read with great interest your interview with Jonathan Lindo III aka Johnny Dollar, Brixton's original baby father. I should know, because I've washed his dirty underpants for more than sixteen years and my side of the story hasn't been heard.

He has at least four children, and I have reason to believe that there are others out there that he doesn't support.

What kind of a man would have all that money and not spend one penny on his pickney? When he abandoned us he took with him the thousands I had invested in his wotless backside over all these years. I know I shouldn't have done it, but what can you do when your baby father says that his life, your relationship together and the future of your family depends on him trying out his latest venture? Now I'm broke. I feel that I have at least a fifty percent share in all his wealth. Yet, even though I am joint owner of everything he possesses until death do us part, I haven't heard a peep from him. If I had demanded to have a nuptial agreement things would have been totally different today. But still, this nuh finish.

Sista Shabazz Nurridin, Brixton.

Baby Father 3: *Does my batty look big in this?*

There were several other similar letters in the magazine from women all claiming that Johnny was the father of their children and that they deserved fifty percent of everything he owned and that they intended to fleece him to get what they deserved.

"But I don't even know who these women are," Johnny protested.

"Are you sure?" Peter Baxter-Smith replied. "Are you absolutely sure?"

Like all the senior partners of the City law firm Baxter, Smith and Mackintosh, Peter Baxter-Smith's hourly rate was too high for anybody but the extremely wealthy to afford. Johnny had arranged a consultation with him over lunch to try to sort out how he should deal with the embarrassing allegations that had appeared every month in *Headwraps* magazine for the last three months. Some of the claims against him were absolutely ridiculous. Like the three dozen claims from different women in Jamaica accusing him of being the father of their children. He hadn't been anywhere near them.

Lesley Lindo, on the other hand, had already filed a paternity suit and was prepared to let her children have blood tests, and could produce numerous witnesses who would testify that Johnny was indeed their father. She could even provide photographic evidence. It wasn't surprising, then, that even his own lawyer didn't quite believe him.

Peter Baxter-Smith knocked back another glass of champagne. That's what he especially liked about his lunch consultations, he got to choose the most expensive restaurants while his clients got to pay.

"And you say that you have no recollection of having fathered children by any of these women?"

"I've told you time and time again, I may have met them, I may have even had a fling with one or two of them at some time or another in the past, I can't remember. But I think I would remember if I had had children with them."

"Have you considered that you might have a medical condition?"

"What do you mean?"

"Well, I remember a case back in Hong Kong when I was living out there, of this chap who woke up one morning and most of his memory had been wiped out. A sad story, he didn't even recognize his own wife and kids."

"Are you suggesting that I've got amnesia?"

"Well…"

"That's absurd. I haven't forgotten who I am, I haven't forgotten my friends, which school I went to. I know who my parents are, and I remember everything in my life very vividly. I think I would have remembered losing my memory."

"That's just my point. You see, this chap could remember certain things perfectly, but other things, things that were too painful for him, had been wiped clearly out of his mind. Selective amnesia they called it."

"I still don't get what that has to do with me. I've

always wanted kids, always wanted to start a family. Having kids would never have been painful to me. I would not have needed to wipe the memory from my mind."

Peter Baxter-Smith could see that his client was not going to accept the possibility, so he moved on.

"Well, unless you can prove otherwise, it looks like you're going to have to part with a large chunk of your money. These women seem to have a very strong case. My advice to you would be to settle out of court. You don't want to leave your vast fortune to the discretion of a judge, do you?"

Johnny kissed his teeth. In his opinion, Peter Baxter-Smith was being paid far too much money per hour to give his clients such naive advice. Why should he settle anything out of court of his hard earned money when he had kept his cock padlocked all this time?

Had he known about the reputation of Judge Deborah Read, Johnny might have thought otherwise. If he had taken a moment to consider the fact that the presiding judge in Lesley's paternity suit against him would be Judge D. Read, he might have had a hint of what was to follow. But since becoming a millionaire, Johnny had developed faith in the British justice system's ability to be fair to the rich much more than it was to the poor.

Being at the other end of an extremely hostile paternity suit can be a very nasty experience, especially when Fate cranks up a kamikaze judge to screw you. The first thing the judge had asked him in court was whether he understood the meaning of the phrase, "I've got you by the balls." Johnny had nodded hesitantly.

"For the record, let it be shown that the defendant understood what it means to have someone by the balls," the judge instructed.

Defendant? Johnny was confused. This wasn't a criminal trial, or so he thought.

Several men had come up against Judge Deborah Read in paternity suits. Each of those several had learnt to their great cost that she was a black woman scorned. Many years before, her first husband had abandoned her with their three kids for a younger woman. Since then she had waged a one-woman campaign against errant fathers. She had won many battles to date, but the war was far from over.

"Right," the judge announced, "this is the settlement of all argument. Which one of you started the confrontation?"

Lesley looked the very essence of the innocent baby mother as she told the story of her years together with Johnny, placing particular emphasis on the fact that she stuck by him even when he "lied, cheated and fathered children by other women."

Gone was the serene Sista Shabazz Nurridin, gone was the princess of the universe. What remained of Lesley Lindo was a woman determined to get what was owed to her, every penny of it.

Judge D. Read wasn't interested in anything that Johnny had to say for himself and hardly gave him a chance to speak. She actually laughed out loud in court when Johnny suggested that, despite the scientific evidence to the contrary and all the other incriminating evidence, this was an unbelievably remarkable case of mistaken identity. "Well, you've got the 'unbelievable' part right," the judge giggled before summing up:

"Jonathan Lindo, better known as Johnny Dollar, the original baby father, you have kept yourself busy producing children wantonly all over the place. It seems your parenting skills end there. It does not surprise me to learn that you are not with any of the mothers and have not paid a penny maintenance. Despite your millions, you allow the good old taxpayer to pick up the bill for your offspring. Someone has got to halt this. I am that someone. Reckless dads like you need government cuts."

Johnny got some cuts all right. It was yet another example of the judiciary being dreadfully unfair to absent fathers. When the judge read out her judgment, Johnny made a quick mental calculation that he would be left with just enough money to pay for the upkeep on his Porsche, but he would have to sell the other cars. He would also have to get rid of the mansion and settle for a small semi-detached without a butler. For a millionaire like himself, that was tantamount to destitution.

What was hidden from the wise and prudent now revealed to the babe and suckling...

Johnny took it pretty badly and he wanted to let everybody know how bad he was feeling. It was clearly a travesty of justice, but all he was concerned with was the possibility of losing everything he had maintained his celibacy for over the last year.

There is nothing quite so distasteful as seeing a

grown man putting himself through public humiliation for the love of money.

"You can't do this to me," Johnny wailed, tears streaming down his face like a waterfall.

"I can and I have," the judge replied coolly.

Miraculously, just as he was about to leave the court and go crying all the way to the bank to arrange an overdraft, Johnny's memory came back to him, as did his patois, and he remembered where he had seen Lesley before. He'd been wrong all along. Of course, she was his childhood sweetheart, the mother of his children, the apple of his eye, the leaseholder of his loins. And now, he wanted her back.

When you really want a woman back, you've got to work hard for it. Lesley was one of those women you had to work hardest for.

"Psssst! Psssst, Lesley, hold on," Johnny called across the courtroom to get her attention. "Joke me ah joke, y'know. Baby, you know me love you bad, mek we leggo the slackness an' feget dis lickle argument yah an' jus' settle an' cool, 'cause it nuh mek no sense you fighting me in court 'bout who seh dis and who don't seh dis from who seh wha'. Skeen? It ah depress me, Lesley, me no lie. It ah depress me. Let's live in one love an' inity an' don't bother with no war or no brutality 'cause, hear wha', this world is like a mirror reflects on what you do and if you smile it will smile back to you."

"So, joke you ah joke?" Lesley sneered. "Well just keep laughing while I take every penny from you. An' if you t'ink me did done, well, me nuh finish...

END... for now